PERCEPTION

Books by Kim Harrington

Clarity
Perception

KIM HA

PERC

RRINGTON

EPTION

A *CLARITY* NOVEL

Point

Library of Congress Cataloging-in-Publication Data

Harrington, Kim, 1974–
Perception : a Clarity novel / Kim Harrington. — 1st ed.
p. cm.
Summary: Trying to decide between her old boyfriend, who betrayed her
but wants her back, and the new boy with whom there are definite sparks,
Cape Cod high school junior and psychic Clare is puzzled by a secret
admirer even as she tries to solve the mystery of a classmate who has
suddenly disappeared.
ISBN 978-0-545-23053-7
[1. Psychic ability—Fiction. 2. Stalking—Fiction. 3. Interpersonal
relations—Fiction. 4. High schools—Fiction. 5. Schools—Fiction. 6.
Cape Cod (Mass.)—Fiction. 7. Mystery and detective stories.] I. Title.

PZ7.H23817Pe 2012
[Fic]—dc22

2011000550

12 11 10 9 8 7 6 5 4 3 2 1   12 13 14 15 16/0

Printed in the U.S.A.   23
First edition, March 2012
Book design by Elizabeth B. Parisi

To Mike.
My better half.

ONE

I STEPPED FORWARD WITH FORCED CONFIDENCE. "Let's do this."

I reached out and took the knife, the wooden handle heavy in my hand. For a moment, it felt like everything in me froze. As if even my blood stopped rushing through my veins.

I thought about the events of the last few days and wished I could have pieced things together sooner. Maybe then, I wouldn't be standing here with a knife and a girl's life in my hands. Every muscle in my body tightened in preparation for what I was about to do.

For what I *had* to do.

I raised the knife above my shoulder. She looked up at me with widened eyes and trembling lips. And with all my strength, I plunged the knife down.

TWO
SIXTEEN DAYS EARLIER

I JUMPED WHEN MY BAGEL POPPED UP FROM THE toaster.

"A bit on edge this morning, are we?" Mom said, buttering her toast.

"Nah. It's quiet in here, and that toaster shoots these things out at warp speed." I plucked the bagel out with my fingertips. "Ouch, ouch, ouch."

"It's hot," Mom said.

"Wow, you *are* psychic!" I joked.

She gently patted me on the face as she brought her plate to the kitchen table. Mom wore a mauve Indian print dress that hung down to her bare feet. Her mass of red curls was tied up in a loose bun. Looking at her was kind of like looking into the future. My mom and I share the same red hair, freckles, blue eyes, and petite frame. Though I definitely won't dress like her when I'm in my forties, unless I fall victim to some midlife personality disorder.

She glanced up from her plate. "Joining me or taking your bagel on the go?"

"I'll join," I said. "I've got some time before school."

"Good, bring the OJ."

I grabbed the jug from the fridge and settled into a wooden chair at the table. "Perry still sleeping?"

Mom grunted in reply.

"Any appointments today?" I asked, quickly changing the subject.

Mom shook her head sadly. I wasn't surprised. It was the end of September and the tourists were gone.

My brother, mother, and I live in a purple Victorian house on the main drag in Eastport, Massachusetts, on Cape Cod. Our family business is in . . . well, entertainment, I guess. The sign outside our home advertises: READINGS BY THE FERN FAMILY. My mother, Starla, is a telepath. She can read minds. My brother, Periwinkle "Perry" Fern, is a medium who can contact the dead.

And me? My full name is Clarity Fern, but I go by Clare. I have a gift called retrocognitive psychometry. I can't predict the future, but I can see the secrets in the past. When I touch an object and concentrate, I can sometimes see visions or feel emotions from when someone else touched the same thing.

Readings can be one-on-one or all three of us working together. Most of our business comes from tourists during the summer months, and we have to budget that money to last throughout the year.

Most townies love it when September comes and the tourists leave for the season. The traffic clears up. The beaches empty. Things slow down. But I've always found it sort of sad. Watching the seasonal businesses close down. The empty lifeguard towers on the beach. Vacancy signs on every motel.

The gray skies that foretold of a long winter to come. Knowing I had months of school and therefore torture ahead of me.

Although things were different this year.

My phone buzzed in the pocket of my jeans, and I slid it out and took a peek. A text from Gabriel Toscano.

Want a ride?

I couldn't help the smile that overtook my face. I typed back.

Sure

"Is it Gabriel?" Mom asked, and I nodded, still grinning.

"Are you dating him?" she pressed on, and I didn't answer.

Steam rose from her teacup, trailed up into the air, and disappeared. Her eyebrows went up and I knew what she was about to do. The thing that made me so angry, I imagined fireworks shooting out of my ears.

She was going to read my mind.

So I focused all my energy on a message and silently repeated it over and over.

Stop invading my privacy, you peeping Mom!

She cocked her head to the side and sighed. "No need to call me names, Clarity."

Almost all mothers are busybodies, always wanting to know every detail of their daughters' lives. I get that. And I was glad Mom wasn't one of those distant, unloving mothers who didn't care enough to bug her kids with questions. But being a telepath gave my mom an unfair advantage and I hated when she used it. If she wanted to know about my love life, she should do what other mothers do: politely ask questions that remain unanswered until the daughter decides to toss her mother a bone over a shared pint of ice cream.

I gulped the last of my OJ as another text came from Gabriel.

Outside now

I pulled back the white lace curtain and peeked out the window. Sure enough, Gabriel's red Jeep was out there idling. He'd already been almost here when he texted me. He knew I'd say yes.

I yelled a "bye" to Mom, slung my black book bag over my shoulder, and darted down the porch steps. I gave a quick wave to Milly, our neighbor, who was crossing the front yard. She often came over to share town gossip with Mom.

I slowed my walk on the driveway, not wanting to appear too excited. Though it was a bright and sunny morning, the fall air was crisp and stung my cheeks. I zipped my gray hoodie, then hitched my jeans up a bit when I realized a slice of stomach was showing.

Not fast enough, apparently. Gabriel's eyes lingered on my midsection a beat too long, then snapped up to my face.

If he were Justin Spellman, my ex-boyfriend turned friend, I'd toss out a snarky remark about staring. But Gabriel and I weren't on those comfortable terms yet. We were still feeling each other out, learning what made each other tick. And Gabriel was a hothead. I never knew when he'd take a comment the wrong way.

Plus, I didn't exactly mind that he was staring.

I climbed into the passenger seat and dropped my bag on the floor. Gabriel fiddled with the radio and I snuck a peek at him. He wore baggy jeans and a white T-shirt that contrasted well against his tanned arms. His black hair was a bit longer than the short cut he'd had over the summer, a little wind-blown with the hint of a curl against his neck.

He stretched his arm over the back of my headrest and leaned toward me. For a moment, I thought he was going in for a kiss, but then I realized he'd put the car into reverse and was just angling to see out the rear window as we backed into the street.

I let out a breath I'd been holding in. Had I wanted him to kiss me again? I didn't know, so I forced the thought out of my mind.

Gabriel and I had met over the summer under intense circumstances. He had just moved to town and was the son of our new detective. When I got involved in the case of a tourist's murder, I was partnered with Gabriel. Much to his dismay.

Years ago, Gabriel's little sister was kidnapped. She'd never been found. His mother had spent all the family's money on psychics. One psychic would say her body was in such-and-such a lake. They'd dredge the lake, nothing. The other would say she was in Bangkok; they'd fly to Bangkok, noth-ing. But his mother kept believing whatever the psychics said, and kept wasting the family's time and money on these wild goose chases. It eventually caused Gabriel's parents' marriage to fail. His mother was constantly drunk now. He and his father moved to Eastport from New York to get some space.

So, naturally, Gabriel had a bit of an issue with psychics.

We had undeniable heat and shared a couple of swoon-worthy kisses over the course of the investigation. But we totally got off on the wrong foot, and I also had an unresolved situation with my ex-boyfriend who didn't want to remain ex.

So Gabriel and I were starting over. Trying to move past our differences and be friends.

Super-complicated friends.

"To what do I owe this honor?" I asked.

"Honor?" he repeated, turning forward and shifting the car into drive.

"Mr. Big Time hot new senior picking up little ol' me for a ride to school?"

The side of his mouth lifted in a half smile. "You think I'm hot?"

"The girls at school do. They even have a nickname for you."

"If it's those vapid blondes who follow you around everywhere, I don't even want to know what it is."

A year ago, the idea of *anyone* following me around would have made me howl with laughter. I was used to attention, but only the negative kind. Being a psychic in a family of paranormal freaks attracts that.

But when I started my junior year of high school a month ago, everything changed. Rather than tell me to get lost as I approached a cafeteria table, people actually asked me to sit next to them. When I walked by, people said, "Hi, Clare," instead of snickering and calling me names.

It was all because of what went down over the summer. My showdown with a murderer, during which I nearly got killed myself, was the talk of the town. It was like I was a celebrity. But I didn't ask for this newfound popularity and I didn't really want it. It wasn't *me* they liked. It was the story. Everyone wanted all the dirty details. How did I feel when the gun was pointed at my head? What was it like when Justin got shot? How did we get the bloodstain out of our hardwood floor?

Believe me, no question was out of bounds to those vultures.

"Okay, I won't repeat the sentiments of any vapid blondes," I replied, laughing. The good thing about Gabriel was you never had to wonder how he felt about anything. He made his opinions painfully clear. Even when I wished he'd keep them to himself. Not because he was wrong. Sometimes I didn't want to listen to him because he was right.

"So who was that old lady going up to your house?" Gabriel asked as we drove down the street. "Is she like . . . a regular customer?"

"No, that was Milly. Our neighbor," I said curtly. I wasn't in the mood for Gabriel's high horse about psychics. He'd finally agreed that, maybe, my family and I weren't frauds looking to bilk grieving people out of their savings. But I knew he still didn't completely approve. One time he'd said that our seeing regular customers was feeding an addiction, like we were drug dealers or casino owners.

I was *not* going to take the bait this time. I gazed out the window at the passing stores and houses.

"What's wrong?" he prodded.

"I don't want to fight with you," I said, crossing my arms.

"Disagreeing and having a bit of back-and-forth is not fighting."

"Bickering, then," I said.

"For it to be bickering, we have to be annoyed with each other." His eyes left the road and instead traveled the length of my body. "And I'm anything but annoyed by you right now."

That was Gabriel's MO. Get me all pissed off, then say something flattering as if that would make it all better.

It usually did.

He parked the Jeep in the school lot and we both got out, causing a few second glances and raised eyebrows as we walked toward the school.

Gabriel leaned closer to me and whispered, "People are staring."

"They shouldn't be," I said, tossing a stern look at a group of sophomore girls. "Everyone knows we're friends."

"Maybe it looks like more than that to them."

"I don't get why it's so interesting. People need to stop theorizing and gossiping about others and focus on themselves," I said with a raised voice.

We'd reached the main doors, but Gabriel stopped walking. I turned to find him staring at me. I'd seen that intense gaze before, but it still started a fire inside me, beginning at my cheeks and spreading everywhere else.

In a low voice, he said, "Everyone in school assumes you and Justin are going to get back together."

I swallowed hard. "And what do you think?"

He stepped up to me and tucked a windblown curl behind my ear. "I think people shouldn't make assumptions." Then he turned and walked into the school.

Just then, Kendra Kiger and Brooke Addison — the so-called vapid blondes — marched up to me. It was good timing since I wasn't sure my legs could move yet and I didn't want to be standing there outside all alone and frozen in place like an idiot.

"What was he saying to you?" Kendra asked breathlessly.

"He is so hot," Brooke said.

"Did he really drive you to school this morning?" Kendra asked.

I nodded. "We're friends."

"So hot," Brooke repeated, staring off into space.

Kendra rolled her eyes at Brooke. "But *why* did he drive you to school today?"

"He offered," I said.

They expected me to jump up and down and squee and giggle about how smokin' Gabriel was, but that's just not me.

I walked into the entrance hallway, which was painted a lovely shade of nursing-home gray. Kendra and Brooke followed closely at my side. I still wasn't used to their company. Kendra, Brooke, and their other friend, Tiffany Desposito, were the most popular girls in my class. All three were blond and pretty, but only Brooke was naturally so. Kendra had to try a bit harder, to overcome the hard angles of her face. Kendra was popular because she had money. Daddy bought her a nice car, and Mommy looked the other way when she wanted to throw parties in the McMansion. Meanwhile, Tiffany rose to the top by being so mean that everyone else was afraid to slight her.

Last year, the only interaction they'd had with me was their daily attempt at verbal torture. But this year, Kendra and Brooke had gotten obsessed with my "magic powers" and desperately wanted me in their clique. I had no interest whatsoever, but I had to admit not being constantly bullied was a nice change of pace.

"Anyway, forget boy talk — we have some news," Brooke said, snapping me out of my thoughts.

It was then that I noticed the buzz surrounding us. Clumps of kids dotted the hallway, leaning in close, whispering and reacting in shocked tones. Something was going on.

"What news?" I asked.

Kendra put on her serious face. "Sierra Waldman is missing."

THREE

"WHO?" I ASKED.

Brooke giggled. "That was my response, too. I don't think anyone knew her."

Kendra added, "She's a senior. New this year. I think she'd been homeschooled or something her whole life." She clucked her tongue. "Only here a month and now she's taken off. Some kids just can't handle public school."

I ignored Kendra's ignorant snap judgment. "How long has she been gone?"

"Apparently a few days, but word only got around today when her mom showed up in the school parking lot, yelling at kids." Kendra's eyes gleamed at the drama of it.

"What was she yelling about?"

Brooke twirled a long strand of blond hair around her finger. "Just asking everyone if they've seen her and all that."

"Does anyone know anything?" I asked, my interest piqued.

"There are a million rumors," Brooke said. "I heard she met a guy online and they ran away together."

"That doesn't make any sense," Kendra snapped. "She'd tell her mom."

"Maybe she knew her mom wouldn't let her go," Brooke said. "Maybe she would have disapproved of her guy. So she left without telling her."

I watched the conversation bounce back and forth like a Ping-Pong game until the homeroom bell rang. I followed the crowd, breaking off to file into our classrooms.

I felt sorry for the teachers who had to repeatedly try to regain control of their morning classes. Especially Mr. Rylander and Mr. Frederick — redirecting attention from juicy gossip to physics and algebra II were almost impossible feats. Sierra's disappearance was all people talked about through the morning and well into lunch. Rumors were spreading like a virus, but no one seemed to have any facts.

I ate my lunch in relative peace, listening to Kendra, Brooke, and the rest of the junior girls around me talking about Sierra. I realized that — for the first time this fall — the spotlight was not on me. And I liked it. Then I felt guilty because it came at the expense of someone else's problems.

I can't win.

But I also felt something else. A stirring inside. Something I hadn't felt since I was brought on board to help the police over the summer. I began to wonder if there was anything I could do to help find Sierra. Then I brushed the thought off. Sierra probably just had a fight with her mother, ran off, and would be back tomorrow.

When lunch ended, I dumped my tray and joined the crowd merging into the hallway, which was plastered with posters about the homecoming dance. I only had five minutes to get to my locker, grab my books, and make it to my next class. The herd was moving a little slow for me to accomplish all of that in time, so I zigged and zagged, apologizing when I accidentally hip-checked a freshman, and finally got to my locker. I spun the dial and started knocking off the numbers.

"They really should give us more time between periods," the girl at the locker beside mine said.

She wore a black T-shirt and a black skirt with fishnets. Her hair was also dyed black, with one bright blue streak on the side that fell in front of her face as she bent down to pick up a dropped notebook. I figured she was new in school. I would have definitely remembered her from last year. There aren't many people at Eastport High who stand out. Standing out is bad. I know this from experience.

"Seriously," I agreed. "It's like they want us to be late. I'm calling it detention entrapment."

She laughed heartily.

"Was it this bad at your old school?" I asked, figuring I'd be nice and reach out.

She straightened. "What do you mean?"

"You're new here, right?"

Her brow furrowed. "No, Clare Fern, I'm not." And with that, she turned on her heel and sped down the hallway.

"Clare, what did you say to her?" Kendra asked, appearing beside me.

"I asked if she was new in school," I said, still confused.

Kendra burst out laughing. "That's Mallory Neely."

Mallory Neely. I knew her, of course. She was the quiet girl, no friends that I knew of. She kept to herself, eyes cast down at all times, and never spoke unless spoken to. She was invisible. I'd actually felt slightly jealous of her in the past because I'd rather have been invisible like her than a big neon flashing bully target.

"I didn't realize it was her," I said.

"Why would you?" Kendra rolled her eyes. "No one notices Mallory. Except this year she shows up looking like a mall goth. Finally wanting some attention, I suppose."

I shrugged. "I think she looks cool."

Kendra bit her lip. This time last year, she'd have called me a freak, and now she wasn't even disagreeing with me. I felt like I'd entered a parallel universe.

"Hey," Kendra whispered, leaning in close to me. "You know the algebra quiz Mr. Frederick is planning?"

"Yeah . . ." I answered warily.

"Why don't you spend a few minutes in his classroom while he's in the teachers' lounge. And . . . you know . . ." She waggled her eyebrows. "See if you can use your powers to get us the answers."

I sighed, not bothering to hide my irritation. "No," I said simply. There were about ten thousand different reasons why I would do no such thing — fear of getting caught being one of them. But Kendra should have known by now I wasn't going to "Dance, Monkey, Dance!" whenever she asked. I wasn't some sideshow at a carnival. She had asked a couple times for me to do a reading of this or that at school. I always refused.

If she truly wanted a reading, she could come to my place of business and pay like everyone else.

"What's up, Kendra," Tiffany said as she approached her locker, almost directly across the hall from mine. She sneered at me and said, "Hey, freak."

Apparently, Tiffany never got the "Clare's cool now" memo. No matter how much her friends supposedly liked me, she never would. Tiffany had always been the one to rally the anti-Clare troops and instigate all devious plans against me. She'd ramped up the torture last year after my brother, Perry, hooked up with her and never called her again. I had to suffer for my brother's man-whore ways. As part of her revenge plot, Tiffany had set her sights on my boyfriend at a party, and Justin had been dumb enough to fall for it. Yeah, alcohol was involved, but that's no excuse. It would take a lot more than tequila to make me lose my virginity to Satan.

"Don't mind her," Kendra whispered into my ear. Then she bolted over to Tiffany, probably to relay the "hilarious" story about how lame Mallory was.

I shook my head and focused on finding my history book. The bell was going to ring any second. I pulled the textbook out and a paper fluttered to the ground. I reached down, expecting to find an old quiz of mine, but it was a note. Written in all caps were three words:

YOU AMAZE ME.

I smiled and my stomach did that little butterfly thing.

And that was when Tiffany screamed.

FOUR

TIFFANY WAS A DRAMA QUEEN, SO LOUD SQUEALS
and other attention-getting techniques weren't unusual for
her. But this wasn't a playful scream. This was an *open your
closet door to find Freddy Krueger, Jason,* and *Michael Myers
hiding in there* scream.

Kendra started screeching, too, while waving her hands in
the air in some crazed dance of ick.

I, along with everyone else in the hall, first froze, then
rushed over to see what had kicked off this performance. On
the floor by Tiffany's locker was a little red box, like what
you'd get with the purchase of some cheap jewelry. It was
flipped over and no contents could be seen. Tiffany had one
hand over her mouth and was pointing repeatedly at the fallen
box with her other.

I reached down and turned it over.

Inside was a cockroach. A large one, in fact. My first
thought was that it must have come from our cafeteria.

"It's dead, Tiffany," I said. "You can stop freaking out now."

"Stop freaking out?" she repeated incredulously. "Someone
put that thing in my locker! Disguised as a present." She

wiped her hands repeatedly on her designer jeans, though I doubt she had even touched the bug.

"It's a prank." I shrugged. "It happens. Believe me. I've found all sorts of things in my locker or scrawled across it."

Tiffany narrowed her eyes. "Is that what this is? Some sick revenge you're taking on me for treating you like the freak you are? You think because Kendra and Brooke have been struck with temporary insanity that you're going to get away with this?" She stepped closer and pointed a finger at me. "Enjoy your little time in the sun now, because soon you'll be crawling back into your loser cave."

"I didn't put the bug in your locker," I hissed. I was about to fill her in on the fact that I wasn't the only one at Eastport High who hated her guts, but before I had the chance, Mr. Frederick stepped out of his math classroom.

"Break it up, girls," he bellowed. Mr. Frederick didn't believe in going bald gracefully. He grew the sides of his hair extra long and then wrapped it around the top, like no one would realize he was just covering up a hairless dome. "Everyone better be off to their classes in three seconds or I'll start handing out detentions like after-dinner mints. Three. Two . . ."

He didn't make it to one. We all scattered like rats, fear of detention pulsing in our veins. At most schools, detention was just another place to do your homework. Not much of a punishment, really, unless you were missing a sports practice or something. In Frederick's detention, however, you were not allowed to do your homework. You had to do additional math assignments. A true punishment.

The rest of my day passed uneventfully until I found myself waiting in the parking lot, watching everyone else hop on school buses or into cars. My brother, Perry, was supposed to pick me up but was clearly running late. So I sat on the curb and fished around in my backpack for the note I'd found in my locker earlier. I read it over again.

It was so sweet. I wished I knew who'd written it. My first thought was Justin. I'd seen him in physics that morning, and he'd smiled at me, but we hadn't had a chance to talk. I knew his handwriting though, and this wasn't it. He could have disguised his writing, of course. But why go through the trouble?

So if it wasn't him ... maybe it was Gabriel. We had shared some serious chemistry that morning. But he knew I wasn't ready to move forward with anything romantic.

Or maybe it was someone I hadn't even considered.

A secret admirer.

Before I could compile a list of suspects, I spied Mallory Neely trudging down the grassy hill behind the school, heading toward the woods. I stuffed the note in my pocket, swung my backpack over my shoulder, and rushed after her.

"Mallory!"

She stopped and turned around, then waited for me to catch up.

"I'm sorry I was such an idiot earlier," I said, slightly out of breath from jogging over to her. "Of course I know you. I just didn't recognize you with your new hair and all that."

She shrugged. "S'okay. I wouldn't expect you to know me anyway. I've always sort of blended in with the walls, you know?"

I looked down at the grass, not sure what to say. Lying to make her feel better would seem fake and lame. So I said, "Well, you don't blend in anymore. I like the new look."

She smiled. "Really?"

"Yeah." I peeked at the woods over her shoulder. "Where are you headed, anyway?"

"I'm walking home. There's a shortcut through the woods that leads to Fennel Street. You live on Rigsdale Road, right? Cutting through would save you some time."

I've walked home plenty, but never taken the shortcut. The woods creeped me out. But they were probably safe with the buddy system and all. Plus, it looked like my brother wasn't coming to pick me up.

"Sure," I said, casting one last glance over my shoulder before we entered the woods.

We followed a well-beaten path that snaked through the trees. It was narrow, with barely enough room for us to walk side by side. The air was thick with damp earthy smells. A pinecone crunched under my foot.

"Fennel Street, huh?" I said, making conversation. "I think someone mentioned at lunch that Sierra Waldman lives there. Do you know her?"

"Sort of."

I waited for her to continue, but she didn't. I added, "Do you think she ran away?"

Mallory shrugged, but didn't look at me. "She's a senior, but she's already eighteen. That makes her an adult. She can do what she wants, I suppose."

"People said some of her stuff is missing, like she packed up and —"

"Don't know," Mallory interrupted. This obviously wasn't a topic she wanted to gab about.

We walked in silence for a minute while I tried desperately to think of something else to say. Anything we might have in common. "You know," I said, "going unnoticed isn't so bad. It's better than being the school freak."

"You're not the freak anymore," Mallory said.

I figured she was referring to my new celebrity status, but then she added, "Because of Justin Spellman."

It was kind of true. When I'd started dating Justin last year, the teasing had let up a bit. But then we broke up, and I was right back where I started from — until the summer's drama.

"He wants to get back together with you, right?" Mallory asked.

"How do you know?"

"Anyone with eyes and ears knows. The way Justin looks at you," she said dreamily. "The way his face lights up when you enter the room. I'd kill for someone to love me that much. You should take him back."

I almost laughed out loud because this was the same conversation I had with myself every time I saw Justin. But the argument always ended the same. "It's not that simple."

"I know what he did. With Tiffany. But doesn't he deserve a second chance?"

"He slept with her," I said. "That's not a small thing."

Justin and I hadn't slept together. I wasn't ready. I dreamed that when it happened, it would be this perfect moment we would remember forever and all that cheesy stuff. But then his first time was on Tiffany's basement couch and he was so drunk he didn't even remember it. That sort of killed the dream for me.

We reached a small stream, wide enough that I wouldn't have been able to jump it. But we didn't have to. A plank of wood served as a little bridge. We gingerly walked single file over it, then fell in step beside each other again.

"What about that new senior, Gabriel Hottie-ano?"

I nearly tripped over a tree root. Gabriel Toscano's nickname sounded so unnatural coming from her.

"Didn't you guys date this summer?" Mallory asked, tucking a blue strand of hair behind her ear.

I stopped and shot her a sideways glance. Maybe she was just awkwardly making conversation, but I was starting to feel weirded out. "You seem to know a lot about me."

Mallory shrugged. "It's a small town. Word gets around."

A twig snapped somewhere in the trees. I turned around to see if someone else was taking the shortcut, but saw no one. Mallory either didn't hear the noise or wasn't fazed by forest sounds.

"We didn't really date," I said, and picked up the pace. "We might have gone that way but . . . it's complicated."

The path emptied onto Fennel, a dead-end street that intersected with Rigsdale, our town's main road and where I lived. The afternoon sun shone brightly, and I squinted as we left the shade of the woods.

Mallory pointed at a small Cape-style house with clapboard siding. "That's me."

"Oh, okay." I was surprised that I'd actually enjoyed our walk. It was nice to talk about girl things. My brother was my best friend, but he didn't want to hear too much about boy problems. And, yeah, I had girls clamoring to be friends with me for the first time in my life, but I wasn't about to share my feelings with the likes of Kendra and Brooke. They'd probably post whatever I said online and tell everyone in school.

I didn't feel that way with Mallory, though. And it was strange because, before today, Mallory and I had never said one word to each other our whole lives. She was probably the only girl at school who'd been lonelier than me.

Maybe this year could be a new start for the both of us.

"So you've got a tough decision, then," Mallory said, stopping at the edge of her driveway.

"About what?"

"Homecoming. It's in two weeks."

"Yeah, I saw the posters at school. What about it?"

"It's Ladies' Choice this year. The girls have to ask the boys." Mallory paused and gave a little smirk. "Everyone knows Justin and Gabriel both want to go with you. So the big question is, who are you going to choose?"

FIVE

I DEFTLY AVOIDED MALLORY'S QUESTION AND MY
conflicted feelings on the topic by claiming to have to hurry
home.

Of course I'd thought about the dance, but I truly didn't
know what I wanted to do. Right now I was leaning toward
skipping the whole mess.

I trudged up the porch steps and opened the front door.
"Perry!"

"In here," he called.

I turned left and entered the kitchen, ready to bitch
him out.

He stood next to the island, smiling sweetly, with a piece
of chocolate in his outstretched hand.

I snatched it and took a bite. "You're not off the hook,
you know."

"I know," he said. "But I figured a chocolate offering
would weaken your wrath."

"Why didn't you pick me up?"

Perry rubbed his right eyebrow, which had a small scar

from when he took a tumble down the staircase as a child. "I forgot?"

It sounded more like a question than an answer, like a lie he was trying on for size. I looked into his eyes, the same icy blue as mine, and knew I couldn't stay mad at him. He'd been through a lot this summer. One minute he was a carefree recent high school grad, always up for a good time or an easy girl. The next minute, one of those easy girls ended up dead and he was the top suspect. In the end, we'd cleared his name, but when something like that happens, you can't snap your fingers and be the same person you were before.

Perry just needed some time. He'd deferred his fall admission to college. Mom and I understood. College could wait a semester. I figured he'd lounge around and play video games all day, and he did some of that, but he wasn't a total lazy-ass. He was also taking an online course in Web design and working on a website for our business. It started out as a basic page but now looked quite professional.

"Where's Mom?" I asked.

"Out buying fabric for those 'dresses' she's making." He made finger quotes in the air and I chuckled.

"So what were you doing that was more important than picking up your little sister?" I popped another piece of chocolate in my mouth.

"I lost track of time." He motioned to his laptop on the kitchen table. "Working on the website."

I took a peek. "Looks cool."

Perry moseyed back to the table. "Milly told Mom that there's a local woman who says her daughter is missing. And she goes to your school. What's up with that?"

I nodded solemnly. "Her name is Sierra Waldman. She's lived here for years but was homeschooled. She's only been in our school for a month. She's a year ahead of me. I don't know much about her at all. But I wish I could help somehow . . ." My voice trailed off as Perry gave me a look.

"Don't even go there," he said, and returned his attention to his computer, effectively tuning me out.

I watched him for a moment. He hadn't inherited Mom's wild red hair and freckles like I had. He had smooth black hair, alabaster skin, and a smile that made tourist girls fall over themselves. He was tall, not a shorty like Mom and me. But he'd never looked lanky before now. I wondered if he was eating enough.

I know everyone deals with trauma their own way and it seemed that Perry's way was to keep it all inside. Mom and I let him do that, since it was what he wanted. And because it was easier than fighting with him and forcing him to talk. But now I wondered if we took the cowardly way out. And maybe Perry was worse off for it.

"What?" he snapped, catching me staring at him.

"Nothing." I wandered back into the foyer.

A loud knock on the front door made me leap back. I opened it with my hand on my heart.

Justin raised his eyebrows. "Dramatic, but I like it. I'm happy to see you, too."

I dropped my hand. "I was walking right by the door when you pounded on it. I'm merely trying not to have a heart attack."

He smiled, his blue eyes dancing. "So you're saying I got your heart racing."

"Incorrigible," I muttered. I opened the door wide, and he stepped inside.

Justin and I were trying on a new label lately: friends. It was a big step for me, considering I despised him a few months ago. For him, I could tell it was a baby step toward our inevitable reunion.

"What's up?" I asked.

"I didn't really see you in school today. You ran off at the end of physics before I could say hi. So I figured I'd stop by to see how your day was." He smiled and slipped his hands in the pockets of his cargo pants. He wore a button-down shirt, white with pink stripes. If any guy could pull off wearing pink, it was Justin.

I looked at him quizzically. "You came here to see how my day was? You could have just called."

"Face time's important. Reminds you that you love me."

"Loved. Past tense." I busied myself with the task of plucking dead leaves from a gigantic plant on the coffee table.

Justin made himself comfortable on the couch. "Anyway, we're friends now. Isn't this what friends do? Don't girlfriends stop by, chitchat about nothing, then change into lingerie, have a pillow fight, and end the day with a session of Truth or Dare?"

I threw a leaf at him, and he caught it in midair. "I wouldn't know."

"Dang," he said. "So you seemed to have your head in the clouds in physics today."

"Yeah," I said. "I was thinking about Sierra Waldman."

"The girl who ran away?" At my nod, he shrugged. "Didn't know her." He stood and began helping me pull the dead leaves. "Your mom really digs flowers, huh?"

"Yeah, it's like a funeral parlor around here sometimes."

"Want me to carry in that big arrangement from the porch?"

I paused. "What are you talking about?"

He ran a hand through his short blond hair. "There's a big basket of flowers out there. You didn't see it?"

I rushed out to the porch and, just like he said, a beautiful arrangement of lilies sat in a wicker basket to the side of the door.

"I would have seen this on my way in," I said. "It must have arrived since I got home. But the delivery guy would have knocked . . ." I spied a little square envelope with my name on it and realized what was going on.

I turned to Justin. "It's very sweet, really. But buying me flowers and leaving me notes isn't going to help you any. I appreciate it, but you have to accept that we're friends and that's it. The only thing that would help your case is a time machine."

I didn't want to sound too mean, so I added, "Thanks, though," as I picked up the basket.

Justin followed me as I brought the flowers back inside, a

confused look on his face. "I'd love to take credit for these beauties, but unfortunately, they're not from me. And . . . what notes?"

As Justin continued his denial, I pulled the square card from the envelope. It bore no name, just the words:

BEAUTIFUL. TALENTED. YOU.

I couldn't help the smile that came to my lips. The heat of a blush bloomed on my cheeks. This was definitely something Justin would do.

"I guess I have some competition," Justin said, reading the card over my shoulder.

I turned to him and raised an eyebrow with suspicion. "This really wasn't you?"

"I swear." He held one hand up and the other over his heart.

Whoever my secret admirer was, he'd left the flowers and snuck away without knocking. He obviously wanted to stay anonymous.

For now.

"Why don't you just do your thing?" Justin asked.

It was worth a try. For my gift to work, I usually had to focus. Which was nice, actually. If I was barraged with visions all day long anytime I touched anything, I'd be in a straitjacket by now.

I held the card in one hand, the little envelope in the other, closed my eyes, and concentrated. I inhaled deeply through my nose and focused on the paper between my fingertips. A minute of silence passed.

"You're cute when you go all psy-chick."

My eyes snapped open.

"Sorry," Justin said. "Did I ruin it?"

"No, I wasn't getting anything anyway."

And that was the frustrating part of my gift. Sometimes it worked and sometimes it didn't. I'm sure there was some scientific basis for it. Like how recently someone had touched the object, or for how long, or whatever. But I didn't know the formula.

"Oh, well. So the homecoming dance is coming up," Justin said, plucking the card from my hand and tossing it over his shoulder. "It's Ladies' Choice."

"Yes, I know," I said, putting one hand on my hip.

He winked. "Just wanted to make sure you knew about it." He looked at his watch. "I should probably get going."

"Okay, see you at school tomorrow. I promise not to ignore you in physics."

I opened the door for him. Instead of walking out, he paused when he reached me.

"Just so we're clear," he said. "If you asked me to be your date . . ." He leaned in, kissed my cheek, and then his lips came up to my ear and whispered, "I'd say yes."

SIX

THE FIRST PERSON I SAW AT SCHOOL THE NEXT DAY was not Justin, but Cody Rowe. Never a good sign.

I turned the corner into the main hallway and saw him standing in front of my locker. He spied me and took off, running right up to Tiffany. The two of them giggled as they disappeared into a classroom.

Someday I'm going to use Cody as evidence in a science experiment to prove nature over nurture, because that kid was born evil. Back in kindergarten, a boy beat him in Candy Land, so Cody held him down on the floor and bit him five times. Even Tiffany was nice in kindergarten. She didn't turn into Beelzebub until she sprouted boobs.

Evil must love company, though, because Cody worshipped Queen Tiffany and performed any demented task she requested of her minion. And it wasn't because he was getting in her pants. No way. Even his athletic prowess couldn't help him in the looks department. And looks were priority numero uno to Tiffany's pants.

I opened my locker, half expecting to find a dead fish or a

pipe bomb. Nothing immediately jumped out at me, so I breathed a little easier. I rifled through my stuff and found nothing. Whatever prank Tiffany and Cody had planned, they hadn't had time to do it. Or maybe he was just coincidentally standing in front of my locker.

Yeah, right.

I pulled out my physics book, shut the locker door, then started in surprise.

Mallory smiled. "Scare ya?"

"Yeah, I wasn't expecting someone to be standing there."

"Sorry." Mallory hefted her messenger bag onto her shoulder. It was bright pink and bore the names of about ten bands I'd never heard of. "So what's up?"

"Heading to physics," I said, and started walking. "You?"

She let out an exaggerated sigh. "Phys ed. The bane of my existence."

"Picked last?"

"Every time. So it's Friday. Got any hot dates tonight?"

I chuckled. "No."

"Come on. You have two interested guys. Pick one and tell me all the deets so I can live vicariously through you."

"Get a date of your own!" I said, chuckling.

"I wish. There is someone I'm thinking of for the Ladies' Choice dance, but . . . we'll see how that goes. What are you up to this weekend?"

I groaned. "It's the first weekend of October. Which means I have hours of Halloween decorating ahead of me."

"Decorating where?"

"Like every room in the house and then the yard. Halloween's my mother's favorite holiday. Plus she feels it's good for business. Like seeing Christmas decorations in the mall makes people want to buy stuff, seeing papier-mâché ghosts in our tree might make people want to talk to the dead."

Normally, I'd be embarrassed revealing so much about my family business, but I felt comfortable with Mallory.

She shrugged. "My mom is addicted to scrapbooking. One entire room in our house is filled with scrapbook crap." She shook her head at the tragedy of it. "We all have our vices."

Kendra ran up, wedged herself between us, and faced me, ignoring Mallory. "Did you hear?"

By the way she was bouncing up and down, she either had exciting gossip or desperately had to pee.

"No," I said. "What's up?"

"The cops are here!" Kendra said it delightedly, like it was good news.

"What for?" Mallory asked, stepping toward us.

Kendra frowned at her and turned toward me, as if I had asked. "It's about Sierra Waldman. Pass it on! I've got to find Brooke and Tiffany!"

She bounced off, and I turned to Mallory, ready to apologize for Kendra's shunning of her. But Mallory's face was turning a light shade of green and I immediately forgot about Kendra.

"Are you okay?" I put a hand on her shoulder.

"No," she croaked, covering her mouth. "I don't feel so good. I've got to go."

I slid into my seat at the black lab table I shared with Brooke, who surprisingly wasn't as annoying on a one-on-one basis as she was when Kendra was around. And over the last month, I'd gotten to know a secret only her lab partner could know.

Brooke wasn't exactly dumb.

When we became lab partners, I shuddered inside, thinking of all the extra work I'd have to do. To my amazement, she handled her own. And she did pretty well on our first test, too, from the peek I'd taken before she stuffed the paper into her bag.

I didn't know why she kept it a secret. Maybe she acted like a bimbo because she thought guys liked it. Or maybe she feared the wrath of Kendra and Tiffany if she were found out. All I knew was, it was one more thing I didn't respect about that crew.

I opened my notebook to a blank page and positioned my pen, ready to take notes on the wonders of physics. My neck tickled a bit and I rubbed it and gave an involuntary shiver.

Someone was watching me.

I glanced to my right, but Brooke was busy fiddling with her mechanical pencil. I turned left, nonchalantly peering over my shoulder, and solved the mystery.

Justin sat in the back row, in his usual seat. His eyes were on me, and when caught, he smiled and gave a little wave. I was about to wave back, but Mr. Rylander startled me with an unnecessarily loud opening to his lecture.

"Magnets!"

I faced forward and grabbed my pen.

"Today we're going to discuss magnets, attraction, repulsion, action at a distance, ferromagnetic material, diamagnetism, and more. It will be on the quiz Monday, so I suggest you all shake out those Friday cobwebs and pay attention."

One person moaned, a few others sighed.

Brooke leaned close and whispered, "Kendra thinks he's cute."

My mouth turned down. "Mr. Rylander?"

I looked up at him while he droned on about north and south poles. He paced back and forth, stopping now and then to push his big black hipster glasses up as they slipped down his nose. His brown hair was disheveled, and he wore jeans and Vans with his shirt and tie. Maybe he would be dorky cute, if he weren't trying so hard to be everyone's friend all the time. Like his mission in life was to be "the cool teacher." He *was* young. He mentioned his age — twenty-three — at least half a dozen times in class. But, in any case, he was a teacher, which made thinking about him that way gross — even for Kendra.

Brooke raised one eyebrow. "And I don't disagree with her."

Apparently, bad taste was contagious.

"What are magnets used for?" Rylander asked.

Some jock answered, "So my mom can hang my A-pluses on the fridge!"

"Anything more likely?" Rylander responded, eliciting a couple laughs.

Brooke raised her hand. "My credit card has a magnetic strip."

"Good. Anything else?" He looked at me.

"A compass?" I said.

"Correct, Clare. Very good." He came around from behind his desk with something in his hands. "Now we're going to do a little experiment showing the principles of magnetism. Let's have Clare come up."

I sighed inwardly. I hated getting up in front of the class with everyone staring at me. My only hope was that most of the kids were in daydream comas by now.

"And," Rylander continued. "Let's see." His eyes scanned the room. "Justin. Please join Clare up here."

Justin popped up from his seat, dashed up the aisle, and stood next to me. I gave him a *kill me now* look with my eyes and he grinned. He knew how much I hated stuff like this.

Rylander stood between us and opened his hands. In each one was a bar magnet. Justin grabbed one, and Rylander offered the other to me.

"Magnets are curious objects," he said to the class. "What's rare about them in the world of nature? Anyone?" After a few moments of silence, he gave up and continued. "They can wield power over other objects without touching them."

He went on for a minute or two about the principles of magnetism, attraction, and repulsion. I stared at the ground and willed time to move faster.

"Okay, Clare and Justin, hold out your magnets."

I tried to forget about the fact that twenty people were staring at me, by focusing on the magnet in Justin's fingers.

"Try to push them together," Rylander said.

Justin and I shuffled closer together and tried to make our magnets connect. It wouldn't work. As much as I pushed it, an invisible force kept them apart.

"They don't want to go together," I said.

"Correct," Rylander said. "They repel each other."

I looked up into Justin's eyes. They were sad, and I wondered if he was thinking about all the terrible things I'd said to him over the past few months. Things I only half meant. Things I said in anger when he'd repulsed me.

"Remember what I said earlier, class. Like poles repel. Unlike poles attract."

I cast my eyes down.

"Justin, you can put your magnet on my desk and return to your seat."

Justin brushed by me on his way, and the skin on our arms met for just a second. But it was enough to give me goose bumps. My skin tingled. It felt electric, from just that brief touch. I rubbed my arm as I watched Justin settle back in his seat, his hand gripping his own arm in the same spot. He smiled knowingly and I turned away.

"Clare," Rylander said, regaining my attention. "Turn your

magnet around so the other pole is aimed at the magnet on my desk."

I did it, glad that I was facing away from the class because I was sure I was blushing.

"Now slowly start to close the distance."

I stepped closer to the desk and held my magnet out, inching my way across the space. Suddenly, Justin's magnet snapped up and latched onto mine.

Rylander beamed. "See what happened? Attraction. Clare didn't even have to put the magnets together herself. The other magnet was unstoppably attracted to hers and pulled over the distance."

I put both magnets back on his desk, then turned to face the class.

Rylander continued, "The magnetic field is invisible, but it can be felt. Did you feel the force when the magnet was drawn to yours, Clare?"

Justin looked at me steadily from the back row.

"Yes," I said softly. "I felt it."

Perry remembered to come pick me up after school, a rare occasion these days for my suddenly hermit brother. I was surprised to find the car waiting and, honestly, a little disappointed. I was hoping to run into Mallory and walk home with her again. I wanted to make sure she was feeling better.

As soon as I got into his little black Civic, Perry shoved the car into gear. We lurched forward.

I planted my hand on the dash. "Easy there, lead foot."

He glared at me. "The least you can do if I'm giving you a ride is not complain about my driving."

"The least I can do?" I scoffed. "Because I'm interrupting you from doing . . . what exactly? Sitting in your room all day fiddling on the computer?" I knew half the time he was working on our website, but still. His attitude rankled me.

He stared at the road, his back almost forcefully straight.

After a minute of silence, I gave in. "I'm sorry, Perry. I've had a craptastic day. I shouldn't have snapped at you."

This was the part where old Perry would have apologized back and we'd punch each other in the arms and laugh, and the fight would be over as quickly as it began. But I was starting to think there was a new Perry.

And he was an asshat.

Instead of replying or at the very least accepting my apology, he gave me the silent treatment the rest of the way home. He gripped the steering wheel so hard his knuckles were white. I thought I saw his eyes bulging out of his head, too.

We pulled into the driveway and he finally seemed to relax. I could almost feel the tension drain from him.

"Clare . . ."

Okay, here's where we'd make up. I smiled and turned toward him.

"I don't think I can pick you up from school anymore."

Not what I was expecting. Was it really that much of a burden to take five minutes out of his day to pick me up? Anger bubbled up inside me.

"Fine," I snapped, grabbing my book bag. "Don't do me any favors!" I slammed the car door and stomped up the porch steps.

I stormed inside and slammed the door, practically in Perry's face. It was immature of me, and I'd basically guaranteed that he'd never give me a ride anywhere ever again, but it felt good. I'd be getting my license soon enough. Then I'd just take the car to school since Perry never left the house anymore anyway.

Perry muttered some naughty words under his breath as he swung open the door, then slammed it shut again.

Mom came out of the reading room with a lit match in her fingers. "What is with all the door slamming?"

"Nothing," I said, turning toward the kitchen.

"Nothing," Perry simultaneously said while climbing the stairs.

"No, no," Mom said, wagging a finger. She blew out the match. "Don't disappear yet. We have a customer coming in a few minutes. She just called."

Perry groaned loudly.

Mom glowered at him, and he shrank back. Yeah, most of the time, she looked like a harmless little hippie, but Mom's glower could make a clam shuck itself.

"Need I remind you that these appointments pay for all the food you gobble up and the Internet connection you're constantly using?" she said.

"I know," he said, and plodded toward the reading room as if he were walking down death row.

I followed him in, less dramatically.

We spent more time on the upkeep and cleaning of the reading room than any other part of the house. It was also the only room that wasn't modernized. From the intricate molding to the oak fireplace, it looked historic. Freshly painted, but historic.

Mom pulled the red velvet drapes closed, and I helped finish lighting the votive candles. Perry kept his head down on the long table.

"So who is it?" I asked.

Mom fiddled with the volume on the New Age music. She preferred it to be very soft, almost unnoticeable. "First-time customer. She didn't leave a name."

The doorbell rang.

"Here she is!" Mom said excitedly. She loved new customers in the off-season. Mostly for their potential of becoming regular customers.

I watched the woman as she walked with Mom from the entryway. She wore nice dress pants, but they were creased, and her white blouse was misbuttoned. Her hair had that finger-in-the-electrical-socket kind of look. Even my bottle of Frizz-Ease couldn't touch that mess.

I stood with my hands folded in front of me, prim and proper. I kicked Perry's chair and he lifted his head up, but didn't stand.

"I'm Starla Fern," Mom began. "This is my daughter, Clarity, and my son, Periwinkle." Mom took a deep breath, about to launch into her script describing our gifts and how our "readings for entertainment" worked. But the woman held a hand up.

"I know who you are," she said in a soft voice. "I live here in town." She paused. "And I read in the paper about what happened this summer."

"Okay," Mom said.

"I'm hoping you can help me. My name is Tracy Waldman. My daughter, Sierra, is dead."

SEVEN

MY KNEES WENT WEAK, AND I SHOT A HAND OUT to brace myself against a chair. I'd never known Sierra Waldman, never spoken to her. She was just another face in the hallway. But to think she was dead . . .

Perry sat frozen, all the color draining from his face.

"They found her?" My voice came out in a croak.

"No," Mrs. Waldman said.

My mother offered her a chair on the opposite side of the table. "Then how do they know she's . . . passed?" Mom asked carefully.

"The police are still claiming she's alive. 'A voluntarily missing adult.'" Sierra's mom made quotes with her fingers as she said the words.

"I'm confused," I said. "Why do you think she's dead?"

"Because I'm her mother and a mother knows." She rubbed her sunken eyes. "She would *not* have run away. If she had a secret boyfriend like in those rumors going around, I would have known about it. She would have told me. Or I would have noticed something." Her voice tightened and she reached a hand to her throat.

Mom sat beside her and placed a gentle touch on her shoulder. "I'm a mother, too. I understand what you're saying. We'll help if we can."

I settled into the chair beside Perry. He hadn't said a word. He seemed to be having a staring contest with one of the candles.

"Our gifts are limited," Mom explained. "But you never know . . ."

"I'm willing to try anything," Mrs. Waldman said. She looked at each of us in turn. "What, specifically, are your abilities?"

Mom spoke first. "I'm probably the least helpful. I'm a telepath. If I concentrate on a person within close range — the same room — I can hear their thoughts. I can't hear past thoughts, only what they're thinking at that very moment. Would you like to try it out?"

Mrs. Waldman nodded eagerly.

Mom closed her eyes and took a deep breath. After a few moments, she began rattling off thoughts as she received them. "We're nicer than you thought we would be. Oh my, she really can do it. It's real. Now you feel bad for your first thought because now we know you had low expectations of us. Now you're wishing I couldn't read your mind —"

"Okay, okay," Mrs. Waldman interrupted, wide-eyed.

"And you also need to use the bathroom," Mom added quickly.

"That's enough," Mrs. Waldman said. "You have proven yourself."

To end the awkward moment, I piped up. "My gift is retrocognitive psychometry. If I touch an object and focus my energy on it, I can sometimes see visions. Nothing in the future. Past only. Connected to that object."

Mrs. Waldman was nodding. "I read about you in the newspaper. About how you helped the police track down that tourist's killer last summer."

Ah yes, the news coverage that turned me into a local celebrity and made me strangely popular at school.

Mrs. Waldman pulled a hairbrush out of her large leather handbag. She placed it gently on the table as if it were an invaluable holy object. "This was Sierra's."

"May I?" I asked.

She gently pushed the brush toward me, and I picked it up. It was forest green, rounded, and obviously well used, from all the frizzy brunette hairs entangled in it. Everyone waited. I closed my eyes, focused on the weight of the brush in my hand, and opened up my mind.

The vision pulsed and appeared from the void. Sierra stood in front of a mirror, brushing her hair. She looked a bit like her mother. The same big unmanageable hair. Shy, downcast eyes. Tall and rail thin. I searched her emotions, but she was only tired. Maybe a bit anxious. I heard the echo of tinny music. Sierra frowned in the mirror, put the brush down, and the vision disappeared.

I opened my eyes and returned the hairbrush to Mrs. Waldman. "I'm sorry," I said. "Just brushing her hair in the mirror."

"Nothing else?" she asked with obvious disappointment.

"Maybe music in the background. Something classical."

Mrs. Waldman smiled sadly. "She was always listening to music. She was a pianist."

I remembered hearing something about that in school. "She won awards and stuff, right?" I asked clumsily, not knowing the correct terminology.

"More than that," she said. "She was a child prodigy. Born special. She could read music at age four. By seven, she was composing."

"Wow, that's amazing." No wonder she kept to herself, I thought. She was writing concertos while the rest of us were still playing with dolls. "I'm sorry I couldn't get anything helpful from the hairbrush."

"Maybe you can come to the house, spend some time in her room?"

I stole a quick glance at Mom, who gave a nod of approval. "Of course," I said.

In the silence, we looked next at Perry, for his turn. His eyes were glazed over, not paying any attention to us.

"My son," Mom said loudly, "is a medium. His gift is perhaps the most powerful, yet also the most inconsistent. If someone who has passed, who is connected to you, is around and wishes to pass on a message, Perry has the ability to hear that message."

Mrs. Waldman paled. "So if Sierra is . . ."

She let her words trail off, but we all knew what she was asking. Mom nodded. We all looked at Perry.

"Does he talk?" Mrs. Waldman asked.

I kicked him under the table, and he blinked rapidly and focused on us. "Sorry. I'm not feeling very well."

"Give it a try, honey," Mom said, her voice filled with sympathy. I was surprised. Normally, any unprofessional behavior gets us verbally spanked, not coddled.

Perry closed his eyes and let his chin fall to his chest. His nostrils flared as he took deep breaths.

"Someone's here," he whispered.

Mrs. Waldman gasped, hand to her heart. I flinched. I suddenly didn't want to be here. Didn't want to watch this poor woman's world fall apart.

"Is it her?" Mrs. Waldman asked, her voice panicked.

Perry, eyes still closed, cocked his head to the side. "No. It's not Sierra."

Mom exhaled her relief so hard, the votive flames flickered. "Who is it, Perry?"

"I'm trying to listen," he said through gritted teeth. "She's hysterical. She's talking too fast, and she's going in and out. I can't understand her."

I wanted to reach a hand out. To comfort him in some way. But I didn't know if it would help or hurt, so I stayed still and watched as he struggled.

Readings didn't take much effort for Mom or me, but they sapped energy from Perry, sometimes leaving him exhausted. Most of the dead visitors people had were elderly. But now he was reaching out for Sierra, an eighteen-year-old girl, the same age Victoria had been. Perhaps it was too much, too soon.

Perry slouched forward and opened his eyes.

"What? Who was it?" Mrs. Waldman asked.

Perry shook his head. "I couldn't understand her, really. She had long blond hair, but that's all I could see. I did get a name, though. Ashley."

Mrs. Waldman straightened. "I don't know any Ashley."

"You have to," Perry said. "I can only contact those who are connected to the place I'm in or the people I'm with. And we have no Ashley connection, right?" He looked at Mom and me. We both shrugged.

"Well, I don't have an Ashley connection, either," Mrs. Waldman said indignantly. She made a face. One I'd seen plenty of times before. Narrowed eyes, scowling mouth. The face of a nonbeliever. She was questioning whether we were frauds after all.

"Thank you for your time," she said, rising, though her voice betrayed her words.

Even after Mom refused to take her payment, the woman's suspicion lingered. And worse, she looked lost and hopeless, as if her last chance had just blown away in the wind.

After Mrs. Waldman left, the three of us went out on the porch. Mom and I sat on the porch swing while Perry sulked in the wicker chair, his chin in his hand.

"I feel so terrible for her," Mom said.

"You listened in more than she gave you permission for, correct?" I asked. Mom had a habit of doing that.

She gave a little shrug. "I wanted to make sure she

wasn't psychotic. Especially if you were going to go to her house."

"I won't be expecting that phone call anytime soon," I said.

Mom nodded. "We didn't live up to her expectations."

I lightly pumped my legs, to give the swing a little push. "Did you learn anything else?"

"She blames herself. Wonders if this wouldn't have happened if she was a better mother. Wonders if she missed anything. She feels powerless."

"I'd like to help her," I said softly.

Mom considered that for a moment, then spoke with a familiar worried tone in her voice. "Clarity, I think we should mind our own business."

"But if we can help a mother find her daughter —" I started.

"We don't know what went on in that house," Mom said, interrupting me. "Maybe that girl is better off wherever she ran to."

"Yeah," Perry said, speaking up for the first time. "It's not our problem."

"We did what we could," Mom said.

My throat felt tight. Solving that case over the summer had planted a seed inside me. And it had started to grow. I didn't want to insult Mom by vocalizing my feelings too much, but readings for tourists weren't enough for me anymore. Entertaining people like I was a circus clown, when I had the ability to do so much more. To *help* people. Working on that case had given me a sense of purpose. A feeling that maybe this ability I was born with wasn't just a freak curse. Maybe it was something more.

I took a deep breath and raised my eyes to my family. "I feel that these gifts we've been given . . ."

"Our abilities?" Mom clarified.

I nodded. "That because we have them, we have a responsibility to use them to help people."

"We do," Mom said. "We make people happy. We amaze them, make their day brighter, their vacations more exciting. And Perry has soothed the grief of dozens of people."

"I know that, but . . . I feel like I should do more."

"Oh, look, it's my little sister," Perry said, breaking into his movie trailer man voice. "She's a sassy girl detective, out to save the world!" I rolled my eyes at his sarcasm, but he continued, "Seriously, Clare. Who do you think you are, Spider-Man?"

I narrowed my eyes at him. "Huh?"

"You know. 'With great power comes great responsibility.'"

At my blank look, he shook his head. "I'm going back inside." His movie man voice echoed as he climbed the stairs. "The sassy girl detective saves the world — one person at a time."

I groaned and balled my hands into fists.

"You know your brother loves you," Mom said. "And you love him."

"Yeah, yeah."

Mom let out a small sigh, got up from the swing, and walked toward the door.

"It's a nice thought, Clarity," she said, "but where would you even start?"

I sat alone for a while, thinking about the Waldmans. It would be helpful to have more details on the case. To make sure I had all the facts.

Maybe from a police source.

EIGHT

YUMMY'S IS THE MOST WIDELY LOVED RESTAURANT in Eastport. Tourists like the kitschy drunken sailor décor. Locals approve of the fresh food. Teens appreciate the prices.

I seated myself in a booth under a precariously hung lobster trap filled with plush lobsters featuring Yummy's logo (on sale for only $12.99 each!). Though the owners liked to stick with the same ocean motif all year round, they *had* placed a pumpkin at the end of the bar. Good for them. Expanding their horizons and all that.

I perused the menu, wondering if I wanted regular dinner or something from their breakfast-all-day menu.

When I'd called Gabriel, asking him if he could pick his father's brain on the Sierra Waldman case for me, he'd asked for dinner at Yummy's in return. I figured he already knew most of the details because . . . what else are you going to talk about with your cop dad at the end of the day? But I'd agreed anyway.

Yummy's was where I first saw Gabriel. I don't believe in

love at first sight, but that day proved the existence of lust at first sight to me.

If Gabriel had come into my life at any other time, I'd have been all over the idea of our being more than friends. If I'd met him before I met Justin. Or even right after the breakup. But now . . . things weren't so simple.

Justin had earned my forgiveness. Hell, he'd nearly died trying to save my life. My feelings for him had morphed and changed again and again, but the one constant was that they never completely went away. I knew I wanted Justin in my life. What I had to figure out was . . . in what way. And I couldn't jump into anything with Gabriel until I answered that question.

I felt a blast of cool fall air as the door opened. Gabriel's gaze swept around the room as he walked in. He wore a faded gray T-shirt, dark jeans, and running shoes. His black hair was choppy and messed up from his habit of running his hands through it. But, still, all the female heads turned. He didn't even have to work at it.

Gabriel's eyes found mine and lit up. My heart did a little dance in my chest.

He slid into the booth opposite me. "Who said there's no such thing as a free lunch?"

"First off, it's dinner. Secondly, it's not free. It's a trade." I leaned forward on my elbows and said conspiratorially, "Information for French fries."

He smirked. "I feel like I'm in a spy movie. Will you be my Bond girl?"

"No, thanks," I said.

He raised an eyebrow. "Why not?"

"All the Bond girls end up dead." I shoved a menu into his hands. "Pick your poison."

We ordered, and I gave voice to something that had been weighing on me. "I have a question," I said. "Did you leave a note in my locker this week?"

"Nope."

"And . . . you didn't happen to leave flowers on my porch?"

He chuckled. "Not my style. It's obviously Justin Spellman."

"I don't think so," I said, fiddling with the zipper on my hoodie.

Gabriel raised an eyebrow. "Do I have another competitor to deal with?"

I waved it off. "Nah, it's probably just a joke."

Our meals came then, and I got down to the real business at hand.

"Why isn't everyone out there looking for Sierra?" I asked. "Amber Alert and everything?"

"It's not like that. She's eighteen, so she's an adult missing person. The protocol is different."

I picked up my sandwich. A clump of lettuce fell to the plate. "How so?"

Gabriel reached for a fry. "Her mother was able to file a report. But Sierra's not high risk because there was no confirmed abduction and no indication the disappearance was not voluntary."

"What do you mean?"

"She took some items, like her laptop and her purse. She also left a note."

A note?! That would have been convenient information for Tracy Waldman to share. "What did it say?"

"'Don't look for me.'"

I leaned back in the booth. "Mrs. Waldman didn't mention that."

Gabriel took a bite of his burger and chewed it slowly. "Well, she wants you to help find her daughter. Wouldn't you be more inclined to look if you thought she was in danger than if you thought she didn't want to be found?"

"Still, I don't like being lied to," I said bitterly.

"Put yourself in her shoes."

I had a hard time doing that, though it was probably easy for Gabriel, considering his family history.

"What do you know about Sierra?" Gabriel asked.

I shrugged. "I didn't know her at all. She'd only been in our school a month. Plus, she's a senior. You probably know more than me."

"Nope. The gossip mill runs on estrogen, not testosterone."

I rolled my eyes and took a sip of soda. "All I know is she was homeschooled for most of her life. She only came to public school this year. She didn't seem to belong to any clique. She mostly kept to herself."

"Is it true that she was some kind of genius?"

"A piano prodigy, yeah. Which doesn't exactly clear a pathway to popularity. It also doesn't make her the type to run away or get into trouble."

"Who knows?" Gabriel said. "It sounds like no one really knew her. Plus, she was so sheltered. Maybe she's rebelling or something."

I shrugged. "So that's it? Because there was a note, the police can't do anything?"

"Even though they're not required to, they did do some follow-up. Her parents are divorced, so they checked into the father, made sure it wasn't a custody thing, even though she's legally an adult. They also went to the school and questioned some kids, though my dad said it seems like she didn't hang with anyone. But that's it unless something else comes up. There's no evidence of a crime and she's not physically or mentally impaired so . . . she's officially voluntarily missing."

I settled back in the booth and mentally sifted through all this newfound information. It sure looked like Sierra had left of her own volition. What would make her write a note like that? Maybe her mother pressured her too much and she wanted to escape. Maybe she was sick of small-town life. Or she got herself into some kind of trouble.

"Ready?" Gabriel asked, plopping a wad of cash down on the bill.

"Hey, this was my treat." I reached out to grab the bill, but he playfully slapped my hand away.

"The treat wasn't the food," he said. "It was the company."

He didn't say it with a wink or any sense of flirtation. He said it matter-of-factly. But it still got my heart racing.

As I stood and followed him toward the door, something peculiar caught my attention. A woman seated in a corner booth had her eyes glued to us. When she saw that I noticed, she lifted a menu up in front of her face.

Odd.

"So what are you going to do?" Gabriel asked, holding the door for me.

I was so disconcerted by the strange woman, I didn't know what he meant at first. Then I realized he was asking about Sierra's mother.

"After Perry's failed reading, she probably thinks we're frauds," I said. "But I'd still like to find a way to help."

He stopped when we reached his Jeep, and turned around. "Good. I'm glad."

I was taken aback by how strongly he said it, and he noticed the surprise on my face.

"I've been there," he said quietly, and he didn't need to explain any further. I knew he was thinking about his little sister and how his parents had been willing to do anything to find her. And this also meant that he believed in me and my ability. He thought I *could* help. I reached out and grabbed his hand, gave it a little squeeze. It wasn't much, but it was all I could offer for now.

Over his shoulder I noticed the door to the restaurant open slightly and a face peer out, then quickly dart back in. The woman again. Watching us.

"Want a ride home?" Gabriel asked.

"No, thanks," I said absently. "Mom dropped me off. She's due to swing by and pick me back up. We're going Halloween decoration shopping. Don't ask."

Gabriel said good-bye and drove off, and I tucked myself

behind an SUV. After a few moments, the woman emerged from the restaurant and hurried over to a small, beat-up car.

I rushed up behind her and tapped her on the shoulder.

She startled and turned around, dropping her keys to the pavement.

"What do you want?" I asked, hands on my hips.

"Nothing. I'm leaving." She picked up her keys and fiddled with them, trying to find the right one.

"Why were you staring at me?"

"I wasn't." She shook her head, but her thick black hair didn't move. Her face was too thin, and dark circles outlined her eyes.

"Why were you staring at my friend?"

She shifted back and forth, a clear tell. It was Gabriel she was following, not me.

"Who are you?" I asked, stepping between her and the car door. At the notion that this stranger might have bad intentions toward Gabriel, a brash courage I didn't realize I had swelled in me.

"It's none of your concern," she said, puffing up her chest.

"If you're stalking my friend, it is my concern."

She eyed me curiously. "You care about him." She stepped closer, but I didn't back off. She considered me for a moment, then spoke. "I'll tell you. If you promise not to tell Gabriel."

She knows his name, I thought in shock. But at her softened voice and demeanor, my alarm subsided a bit. Still, I felt protective. I wasn't going to keep anything from Gabriel that he should know. At the same time, I wanted to hear what her deal was.

"I can't promise not to tell him," I said. "It all depends."

The woman nodded. "Maybe you'll agree after you've heard what I have to say."

"Okay."

"I am Aleta Toscano. Gabriel's mother."

NINE

MY MOUTH OPENED.

Way to go, Clare. Way to impress the mother of a prospective boyfriend. Moms love their boys to date psycho overprotective girls.

"Gabriel doesn't know I'm in town," his mother said.

Now that I knew who she was, I was surprised I didn't notice the resemblance earlier. She had Gabriel's eyes.

Those eyes pleaded with me as she continued, "His father doesn't, either. I have a room in a hotel. I only arrived today. When I saw my son in the restaurant, I hid because I didn't want our first meeting in months to be in a place like that. I want to approach him at the right time, in the right place. We have a lot to talk about."

I nodded slowly, words suddenly failing me.

She tilted her head to the side. "Are you my son's . . . girlfriend?"

"No," I said, wringing my hands. "We're just friends."

She smiled. "He's lucky to have a friend like you looking out for him."

I returned her smile nervously. "Thanks. I won't tell him,

Mrs. Toscano. You have the right to approach him however you want."

"Thank you . . . Miss . . ."

"Clare."

"Thank you, Clare."

She held her hand out and I shook it, despite the gnawing feeling that things were about to drastically change.

On Saturday, Mom — like a woman possessed — went shopping for even more decorations. Perry was bogarting the television. So I decided what better way to spend a Saturday than with homework.

Normal teens do their homework on Sunday nights. I realize this. I am not normal.

I hate procrastinating, so much so that I often do my homework on Friday so it won't be hanging over my head all weekend long. The good thing is, my (nonexistent) social life doesn't usually interfere with this quirk of mine.

Before I settled in to write my paper on the causes of World War II, I checked my email.

One new message.

From mybeautifulClare. Subject line: empty.

My heart sped up. Was my secret admirer going to reveal himself? The cursor hovered over the message. I wanted to know who it was, but felt conflicting feelings on who I *wanted* it to be. If it was Gabriel or Justin, then it was a nice effort but didn't help the stalemate much. If it was someone new . . . then I suppose my reaction would depend on who it was.

But did I need any further complications in my romantic life? Especially with all the pressure surrounding that stupid dance?

I told myself to shut up and just open the email. I clicked.

I hope you liked my flowers. You deserve to be lavished with gifts. Because you are unique. You are special.

Still anonymous.

I read it over three or four times. The note in my locker and the flowers had made my stomach do little flips over the unexpected flattery. But now I felt a bit nervous. The email was all complimentary. There was nothing threatening about it. But it didn't seem right. I hemmed and hawed for a few minutes about whether or not to write back and finally decided to do it.

Thanks for the compliments, but I'm at the point now where I want to know who you are. Please tell me.

I hit SEND, and only a minute later, I got a mailbox error in return. The email address did not exist.

Someone had created the address at one of those free mail websites, used it once to email me, and then deleted the account.

Strange.

Wouldn't he want to know my response to his email? Wouldn't he want to know how I felt about his advances? Whether I was interested?

Obviously not.

But why?

Two scenarios formed in my mind.

Maybe he never planned on telling me who he was, never intended on going past the secret admirer thing. Either because he was a harmless guy who was afraid of rejection or there was no secret crush and it was someone playing a joke on me.

The other possible scenario was a bit darker. He *did* want to take this out of secrecy and to the next level. But he didn't care about my response because it didn't matter how I felt. It didn't matter whether I wanted him or not. Because he was going to have me either way.

I shuddered, then tried to talk myself off the ceiling. I had no evidence for the creepy scenario. This secret admirer had been nothing but nice. I'd just learned to expect the worst in people. Or I'd been watching too many crime dramas with my mother.

The instant messenger window popped up with a loud *bing*.

MALLORYNEENEE: what's up?

I typed back:

REDFERN: Mallory?
MALLORYNEENEE: yeah. when I was little, I couldn't say Neely, so I said my name was Mallory Nee Nee. wasn't I cute?
REDFERN: how did you get my IM?

MALLORYNEENEE: I'm a clever girl. so your handle . . . from the book?

REDFERN: no, from my hair and my name. how are you feeling?

The last time I'd seen her, she looked like she was going to blow chunks in the school hallway.

MALLORYNEENEE: I'm fine. so you got a hot date tonight?

REDFERN: no. decorating. plus, boys = complicated. we've been through this.

MALLORYNEENEE: you only have a few days to ask one of them to go to the dance. you'd better pick one and lock that down.

REDFERN: I might have a third option . . .

MALLORYNEENEE: do tell!

REDFERN: secret admirer. left a note in my locker, left me flowers, now just sent me an anonymous email.

MALLORYNEENEE: that's cool, right?

REDFERN: I thought so at first, but now I'm getting frustrated. he should just tell me who he is already.

There was a long pause.

MALLORYNEENEE: but what would be the fun in that?

I was about to compose a response when she quickly typed:

MALLORYNEENEE: gotta go

And signed off.

TEN

I HEFTED THE LAST SHOPPING BAG FROM THE trunk, carried it into the house, and dropped it on the floor.

"Careful, Clarity!" Mom said, rushing over to the bag. "This one has the crystal pumpkin in it."

"It's fine. They wrapped it in, like, ten thousand layers of tissue paper." I collapsed onto the couch and scanned the chaos. Witches, pumpkins, and ghosts of the papier-mâché and ceramic variety littered the floor.

Mom stood with her arms crossed, tapping her foot. "I brought everything up from the basement, but we're missing something."

"How can you even tell?"

She ignored me and stared at the spooky mess. "I've got it!" She lifted her finger in the air. "The witch crash. Where's the witch crash?"

I groaned. That particular decoration was one we'd bought many years ago. When hooked onto a tree, it looked like a witch on her broom had crashed in our front yard. We got a ton of laughs from it the first year, then everyone started copying us, and now I despised it.

"That thing is so cheesy. It would be a blessing if we lost it."

Mom ignored my complaint. "I think it's in the attic. Will you be a dear and go get it?"

"What about Perry? Make him do it." I realized I was whining, but I hated the dusty, dark attic.

"Perry is uploading a new page to our website with our pricing changes. Unless you can do that, get your butt up there." She shooed me off the couch with her hands and I dragged myself up the stairs.

The attic door is in the ceiling of our second-floor hallway. I yanked the rope and unfolded the stairs. I gave them a push or two to make sure they were still solid and climbed up.

I feebly reached out in the dark for the pull chain of our sole lightbulb and jerked back in surprise as it hit me on the forehead. I tugged it, and sighed in relief when the light went on. The thick dusty air tickled my throat. I tiptoed across the plywood and beams, and scanned the cardboard boxes labeled with black marker. Mom kept way too much of our school junk. When were we ever going to need something from the *Perry Third Grade* box? But, in a way, it was sweet.

I had no idea where the stupid witch could be. There were no more boxes marked *Halloween*. Maybe she'd been accidentally tossed into a Christmas one. I was about to give up when I noticed an unmarked box in the corner. The dust had been disturbed around it, as if someone had recently sat next to it. I shrugged and did the same.

The box was empty, except for one thing at the bottom. It looked like an old flannel shirt, red and black. Definitely not

Mom's style. I picked it up and realized something was wrapped inside. I slowly unfolded the shirt, undoubtedly of the men's variety, and found a framed photo of Perry and Mom. They were standing in front of the house, holding hands.

Wait.

Mom looked young in the picture. Too young to be standing with a full-grown Perry. I looked closer and realized it wasn't Perry at all.

It was Dad.

I didn't know from memory. I was only a year old when my father left us. But I knew in my gut this was him.

I'd heard a couple times from others that Perry looked a lot like our father. But only now did I realize how much. I wondered how it must feel for Mom, to see Perry every day and be constantly reminded of the man she loved and lost. No wonder she hadn't moved on.

When we were younger, Perry and I would sometimes ask about our father. The only answer we got was that he left. We never knew why. But we saw how much it hurt Mom to talk about him, so we stopped asking, out of love for her.

All I knew about our dad was that he and Mom had grown up in the same town, a spiritualist community in western Massachusetts. Most of the inhabitants were paranormally gifted and they tended to marry each other to pass on the genes. Mom and Dad married, moved out to the Cape, bought this house, had Perry and me, and then . . . I don't know. The rest is a blank.

I traced my finger down his face in the picture and wondered. Did he have another family now? Was he even alive?

I'd never felt my father's absence. It was probably for the best that I was too young to remember him. How can you miss what you never had? Between Perry and Mom, I'd grown up with more than enough love. I didn't need Dad.

But still, looking at his picture, I felt something stirring inside. A strange little ache.

Footsteps on the attic stairs alerted me that someone was coming up. I quickly rewrapped the photo and put it back in the box. I didn't want Mom to see that I'd found it. If she did, it would probably disappear like all the other evidence that my father had ever existed. I struggled with the flaps on the box top. I almost had it closed.

"What are you doing?"

I whipped around and exhaled my relief as I saw the head poking up into the attic. "Oh, hey, Nate."

Nate Garrick is my brother's best friend and, to be honest, one of my best friends, too. He'd been as much a fixture in my life as if he'd been a second brother.

He climbed the last stair and walked toward me, slightly hunched so he wouldn't bang his head on a beam. "Do you need help carrying anything down?"

"Thanks, but I can't even find the damn thing." I stood, wiping my dusty hands on my jeans.

"What are you looking for?"

"That witch crash decoration we put on the tree in the front yard every year."

"You mean that?" Nate pointed at something up and over my shoulder.

I turned around and there it was, hanging from a rafter on a hook, the witch's legs dangling. I shook my head. "I can't believe I didn't see it hanging up there. I'm a moron."

He waved me off. "Ah, you were probably looking down at all the boxes, not up."

"And you're just being nice."

He smiled brightly. "That, too."

"So how's college?" I asked, pulling the witch down.

"It's good." He shoved his hands in the front pocket of his Red Sox sweatshirt.

"Haven't you come home, like, every weekend since you started last month?"

Nate shrugged. "It's only Boston. It's not that far away."

"That's not what I mean. Don't you want to stay there and party? Meet girls? Go all Animal House?"

Nate smiled. "I do that every night during the week. Weekends are my time to come home and relax."

That had as much chance of being true as Perry entering a seminary. Not that Nate was *too* serious. He had a great sense of humor and could have fun, but he was shy around people he didn't know, especially girls. He'd been a gangly boy and a lanky tween, as if his height grew too fast for his frame. But now he was filling out, and I was sure his body, plus those dynamite green eyes, caught the attention of a few coeds. But Nate just wasn't the girl-juggling type. He always claimed he was waiting for the right one. He was like the anti-Perry.

Still, I wondered if he was enjoying college as much as he let on. I worried about him.

"Seriously, Nate. What gives?"

His shoulders slumped forward a bit and he lowered his voice. "Perry's my best friend, and I think he needs me right now. The keg parties can wait."

That was just like Nate. It wasn't his fault Perry chose to defer a semester and lock himself in his room. And Nate could forget about it, say it wasn't his problem, and party it up at school. But instead, he was coming to visit here every weekend. Not because Perry asked him to come, but because he knew Perry needed a friend around.

"You're one of the good ones, Nate," I said.

He blushed and shuffled his feet. "You all set up here?"

I put the witch under my arm and nodded. "I'll follow you back down."

When we got downstairs, Nate left to have dinner with his family, but I was thankful for his brief visit. Even if he only stopped by for an hour, it always brightened Perry's mood. Perry was happily helping out now, busy putting orange LED-lit faux votive candles in every window.

I headed outside to finish with the few outdoor decorations Mom hadn't had a chance to take care of. It was surprisingly warm, but I still wasn't used to how early darkness was falling this week. I turned on the outside porch light to help me see better. Dead leaves crunched under my feet as I crossed the yard.

I surveyed what I had left to do and chose a lawn sign. It was wooden, hand-painted, with a ghost that said, BOO TO

YOU. I picked up the mallet, ready to hammer the sign's stake into the ground, when I first felt it. That prickly, creepy, familiar feeling.

I was being watched.

I scanned the windows, all lit but all empty. I faced our neighbor Milly's house and saw nothing. Then I turned toward the small patch of trees on the other side of our property. I squinted at the shadows. The unmistakable feeling of unseen eyes weighed on me.

Someone was out there, in the darkness. I knew it. I strained my eyes, but couldn't see anyone.

After a few moments of silence, I turned back to my work, aiming the mallet at the sign. Then came a sound. A scrape, like a shoe on the ground.

I spun around, eyes narrowed at the gloom. I waited, but heard no other sounds. Not even natural ones. Like the night was holding its breath. I still felt the presence, the tingling feeling on my skin. The mild fall evening suddenly felt very cold.

I was frozen in place with indecision. Running inside would feel cowardly, like I was letting whoever was watching me win. But every nerve in my body was telling me to go. I compromised by standing still for one more minute, then slowly backing toward the house. As my foot hit the bottom step of the front porch, I saw movement from behind a tree in the neighboring yard. A person was walking fast, headed my way. I balled one hand into a fist, tightened the other on the mallet, and readied a scream.

ELEVEN

THE SHADOW CAME CLOSER AND FORMED A FAMILIAR frame. It was a girl.

"Clare!" the person called out.

I stepped forward, but kept the mallet gripped tightly in my sweaty palm. "Mallory?"

Finally she was in the porch light's reach. "Hey, what's up?"

I eyed her with suspicion. "Were you standing out there watching me in the dark?"

Mallory's brow creased. "Uh, no, I just walked here from my house. Figured I'd help you decorate. You said you had a lot of work to do."

I paused, not quite sure whether or not I believed her. But it was true that I'd complained about all the decorating.

"Why would I stand and watch you?" Mallory asked, frowning. "That's creepy."

I shook my head. "You're right. Sorry. I'm sure there was no one there. This secret admirer just has me imagining things." I felt bad for suspecting her. She was just coming over to help.

"So you're feeling better?" I asked. "When I last saw you at school, you were green."

"Oh yeah. Totally fine."

I hammered the sign into the lawn. "Did you know Sierra well?"

"What?" Mallory's eyes widened.

"That's why you felt sick, right? Because the police came to school to ask around about her?"

"No, not at all. It was . . . something I ate," she muttered as she sorted through the decorations.

I got the feeling Mallory was lying, so I pressed on. "But you live right near her, you must have —"

"Oh! Look at this one!" Mallory picked up a giant inflatable pumpkin.

"Yeah, the problem is we can't find our air pump."

"I'll blow it up."

I shook my head. "That would take forever."

"I don't mind." She pulled at the spout. "My folks always say I'm full of hot air."

I rolled my eyes and giggled at her dumb joke. While she nearly hyperventilated blowing up the pumpkin, I worked on the rest of the decorations. We gabbed about TV shows and I even confessed my love for horror movies, something I didn't tell most girls, who might think that was a weird thing to like. Surprisingly, Mallory loved them, too, and we gushed about our favorites and argued over the greatest of all time. My vote went to *Poltergeist*. Hers to *The Shining*.

"This was fun," I said when we'd finished. "Thanks for coming."

"No problem." She stood and surveyed our work. "Hey, what are you doing tomorrow?"

I only had to think for a second. "Nothing."

"Good!"

"Why?" I wondered if I would regret this.

She grinned wickedly. "Because we're going dress shopping."

Mallory's house was small and cluttered. Not in a dirty, hoarders kind of way. More like a family who loved and lived their hobbies.

"Where are your parents?" I asked.

"They're out buying stuff that will be in our yard sale next summer." At the sight of my confused face, Mallory added, "They're antiquing."

I laughed, finally getting the joke.

"As you can see, my mother is a big reader." Mallory made a sweeping motion with her hand at the several piles of books in the living room. "And my father is a photographer." Her fingers trailed along several framed photos on the wall, knocking one off center.

I stopped and fixed it. Symmetry was a compulsion of mine. When I was sure the frame was once again level, I gazed at the picture itself, a black-and-white landscape of the beach in winter.

"I love this," I said.

Mallory's face lit up. "I took that one."

"Really?" I looked at her and back at the photo. "You're pretty talented."

"Thanks." She smiled smugly. "I might try to join the yearbook staff this year."

"They'd be lucky to have you."

The egg timer dinged in the kitchen and Mallory raised her arms in victory. "The pizzas are ready! We'll chow and then stuff our bodies into tight dresses."

"*You* will," I corrected. I'd made Mallory agree to some concessions about our alleged dress shopping trip. First, we'd have a fun lunch before we went. Mallory suggested make-our-own-pizzas at her house, which was cool by me. And second, I wasn't trying on a thing. I'd come along and help her find a dress for the dance, but that was it.

Mallory pulled the mini pizzas out of the oven and the smell filled the kitchen. I had chosen to make the old faithful: pepperoni. But Mallory took a more precarious route with her concoction. I frowned as she cut hers into slices.

She laughed. "Are you making faces at my pizza? You're going to hurt its feelings."

"I'm all for trying new things and all, but pickles? On a pizza?"

"It's good, I swear!" She slid a slice onto her plate as I scooched my chair closer to the island. "Want a bite?"

I shook my head quickly. "No way. I'm sticking with mine." I took a bite and chewed slowly. It was pretty darn good for homemade pizza.

I watched as Mallory took the first bite of hers. Her eyes rolled back into her head and she moaned, pounding the table with her fist.

"What are you doing?" I said, laughing.

"Don't interrupt me, I'm having a flavorgasm."

That killed it. I cracked up, which kicked off a stream of laughter from Mallory in return. It was infectious, and soon we were both doubled over. After several minutes and tears in our eyes, I was finally able to breathe again.

Who knew that this strange girl I'd never spoken to before this month was so funny? Behind all that shyness, Mallory had hidden a hilarious personality.

"What?" Mallory asked, eyeing me suspiciously.

"Nothing."

"Tell Mama the truth now, and you won't get in trouble."

I shrugged. "You're just not what I expected, that's all."

"What did you expect me to be? Mute?"

I snorted. "Not exactly. Maybe a bit boring."

Mallory waved her hand dismissively. "I'd give you the lecture on judging, books, and covers, but I think you've lived that one."

"Oh yeah. People expect me to go into trances, dress like my mother, and talk about woo-woo all the time." I paused, slice of pizza held in midair. "I'm glad we became friends. I'm glad that, as jaded as I am, someone can still surprise me."

Mallory looked down at her plate. I'd complimented her, but for some reason she looked . . . sad. We finished eating in an uncomfortable silence, until Mallory brought our empty plates to the sink and announced, "Dress time!"

I moaned at her enthusiasm, which made her laugh. I was glad the tone had become lighthearted again. I followed her outside and into a silver sedan.

"Nice car."

Mallory chortled. "I don't have a car. This is my mom's. Normally they would never let me take it out — I just got my license. But I think my mom was so deliriously happy at the idea of me doing something normal — like dress shopping — with an actual, real-life friend from school, that she let me take it."

"I know how that is," I said. "Now that girls at school are scrambling to be my fake friends, my mom's all 'You should at least *try* being sociable, Clarity. You might like it.'"

We shared a laugh at my mom imitation.

After a few minutes, I noticed we weren't headed in the right direction. "Aren't we going to the mall?"

"Not unless we want to look like one of the Barbie Brigade. We're going to Lorelei's."

I think I'd walked by the storefront once. I'd assumed it was a costume shop. "What do they sell?"

She gave me a sly glance. "Renaissance, medieval, Victorian, and vintage dresses."

Oh, dear lord.

We entered the store, and my senses were immediately overloaded. The music was loud and jarring. The smell of incense permeated the air. And the lighting was so dim that my pupils expanded to the size of dinner plates.

"Welcome to Lorelei's." A saleslady glided up to us. She had white foundation pancaked on her skin, and went heavy on the eyeliner and red lipstick. She wore a corset that barely contained . . . I'm gonna say it . . . her swelling bosom. If she had to sneeze, I was covering my eyes because even a slight cough could pop one of those suckers free.

Mallory had already started rifling through the racks oohing and aahing at various pieces. She pulled out a black satin, floor-length gown embellished with crystals along the bust. "Definitely trying that one on." Then she picked another black gown, this one formfitting and laced down the back.

"We have some elbow-length black leather gloves that go perfectly with that one," the saleslady said.

I slowly flipped through a rack. Ninety-nine percent of it wasn't my style, but there were a few that weren't so bad. Too bad they were so pricey.

"I don't understand why you want to go to the dance anyway," I said.

"This is my year of trying new things." Mallory pointed to her dyed hair and funky clothes. "See exhibits A and B." She smiled and gave a little shrug. "I've never been to a dance before and I'm a junior. It's, like, this rite of passage I feel like I should experience. Plus, it might be fun."

"Did you ask anyone to go with you yet?" I asked.

"No, but I could always go alone. Or with a friend." She looked at me pleadingly.

I mock-glared back. "Who are you thinking of asking?"

"I don't know," she answered quickly. "So who's the Barbie Brigade taking to the dance? They must have mentioned it to you."

My eyes rolled up to the ceiling as I tried to remember the lunchtime chatter. "Brooke's bringing Jordan, I think. Though they make up and break up every week. Kendra wants to ask

Brendan, but she hasn't yet. I don't know the rest. To be honest, I only half listen to them."

"That's half more than I would," Mallory said, lifting another dress from the rack. This one had black netting over blue satin. "I think I have enough to try on." She frowned at my empty hands. "Where's yours? Can't find anything you like?"

"Honestly, I can't afford anything here, and I don't even know if I'm going to the dance."

Mallory pulled a dress from the rack. "Here, try this on."

"No, I —"

She shoved it into my arms. "Even if you're not buying, you have to play dress-up with me." She glanced down at the random dress she'd grabbed and added in surprise, "And that pale green really works with your hair."

I held it up in the mirror and had to admit she was right. It was my style, too. Simple, knee-length with spaghetti straps. But it was also glamorous in its simplicity — kind of Old Hollywood. I snuck a peek at the price tag, and audibly gasped.

"It's vintage," the saleslady said. I hadn't even realized she was still watching.

"It couldn't hurt to try it on," I said with a shrug. Even if I couldn't afford to buy it.

Mallory gave a little clap. We each took a dressing room and busied ourselves as the sounds of zippers and rustling fabric floated around us.

"Clare," Mallory said minutes later. "Come out and tell me what you think. I love this one!"

I peeked my head out the crack of the door and watched her spin. She wore the blue one with the black lace over it. No, not blue. Indigo. It was perfect for her — beautiful, yet also unusual.

"I love it. Honestly, Mallory. It's gorgeous."

"I know, right?" She beamed. "Now you come out. I want to see yours."

I opened the door and tiptoed out, feeling overexposed. I crossed my arms and rubbed my shoulders.

Mallory's eyes widened and she covered her mouth. "It's like it was made for you."

The saleslady wandered over and suggested we head toward the bay of mirrors near the front of the store, to see our dresses in the natural light. Mallory rushed forward, pulling me behind her. I felt even more naked there, by the giant storefront window with pedestrians walking by. But the dress looked even better.

"Damn, Clare. You've been hiding a cute little body underneath those big hoodies," Mallory said.

I couldn't help but smile. The dress really did look fantastic. But it was out of my price range and would just hang in my closet since I didn't plan on going to the dance. So despite Mallory's boos and hisses, I went back to the dressing room, changed, and put the dress back.

Minutes later, returned to my comfortable jeans and tee, I went along with Mallory to the register.

"I can't believe you didn't buy it," she said with a pout.

"I don't know if I'm going," I repeated.

"If you don't, it's going to totally suck."

"You'll do fine without me," I said.

The saleslady swiped Mallory's credit card with a big commission-induced smile. "She's right. You'll look beautiful at the dance. You already caught someone's eye."

"What do you mean?" I asked. A spidery tingling crept down the back of my neck.

"When you went back to the dressing rooms, another customer came over to me all concerned because some guy had been ogling you two through the storefront window. Kind of clandestine-like from behind the pole."

TWELVE

"EW! PERV!" MALLORY SAID.

Dread swelled in my stomach. Yeah, it might have been just some stranger checking out girls in their dresses. Or it could have been my secret admirer. Following me.

"What did he look like?" I asked.

"I didn't ask," the saleswoman said, putting a pen and the receipt on the counter for Mallory to sign.

"Where's the customer who saw him?" I pressed.

"Long gone." She slapped the credit card back on the counter. "Listen, girls, take it as a compliment. And enjoy it while you can. Youth is fleeting. When you're my age, you'd give anything to have someone ogle you."

Mallory didn't seem too concerned on the way home. She said she figured it was a random person who happened to be walking by, not a stalker or anything. And that was a reasonable argument, but try telling that to my intuition.

She dropped me off at home and sped away. No cars were in the driveway. I tried the knob. Locked. On my way out, I hadn't brought my key, figuring the chances of both Mom and Perry being out were the same as Tiffany becoming my

BFF. Thankfully, we kept an extra key hidden under a potted plant on the porch.

I let myself in and flopped onto the couch, every sound I made echoing in the quiet. I got up on my knees and peeked out the window like a dog waiting for its owner. The driveway stayed empty. There had been times when I'd have paid money to have the house to myself like this. But now I wanted someone to talk to.

I felt so much pressure about this stupid dance. From Mallory. And from Justin and Gabriel. I knew it wasn't fair for me to keep both guys hanging on. But I wasn't, really. They could date whoever they wanted. I didn't tell either one of them to wait for me. But, at the same time, I didn't want to be rushed into making a choice. I wanted to explore friendships with both of them, and figured a romance would organically grow when I was ready.

It would be so much better to have someone to talk this out with, but I had no one. If I complained to Mallory about the pain of choosing between two hot guys, she'd roll her eyes and make some sarcastic comment about those being great problems to have. If I tried to talk it out with Mom, she'd just give me garbage about how my inner self already knew the answers and I just needed to listen.

Believe me, I've tried that. Apparently my inner self is mute.

I was about to give inner Clare another go when I heard a sound. A creak from upstairs. Then another. Like footsteps.

I shot up from the couch and stood at the bottom of the staircase, listening so hard I wasn't even breathing. Another shuffling sound came from around Perry's room.

I bolted into the kitchen and grabbed a large knife from the drawer. Then I grabbed the cordless phone. I dialed 9, 1, and held it with my finger on the 1 while I raised the knife in my other hand. Icy fear raced through me as I quietly climbed the stairs. I peeked down the hallway. The door to Perry's room was slightly ajar. I crept up to it, heart pumping madly with adrenaline, phone and knife at the ready. I took a deep breath and kicked it open.

Perry screamed.

I screamed.

"What are you doing?" Perry yelled.

"What are *you* doing?" I shouted back.

"You're the one with the knife and the —" He raised an eyebrow. "What were you going to do, beat me with the cordless?"

I glanced up at the phone raised high. I sighed and laid them both on his desk. "Your car isn't in the driveway."

"So? Nate took it out to get us some food. Why would you make the leap to a psycho killer hanging out in my room? Jumpy much?"

"It's just . . ." I dragged my hands through my hair. "I'm a little wired because I've been getting these anonymous notes."

He leaned forward, eyes narrowed. "Threatening you?"

"No, complimenting actually. But —"

Perry shook his head, his brotherly worries gone. "You seriously need to stop watching all those horror movies. You nearly stabbed me because you have a secret admirer?"

My face flushed with embarrassment. "Sorry."

Perry looked back at his laptop, his concentration easily returning.

"What are you up to?" I peered over his shoulder.

"Homework for my online class."

His online class. When he should be out in a real-world class. In college.

I sat down on Perry's bed and rested my chin in my hands. "Can we talk about what we haven't been talking about?"

Perry tilted his chair backward and propped his feet on the desk, crossing them at the ankles. "I'm sure Mom would do a better job than you with the birds-and-bees talk."

"Perry, be serious. I'm worried about you. And don't do your usual thing."

"What's that?"

"Act like a jerk, then storm off."

"A jerk?" He brought his feet down off the desk.

"I know that's not who you are; it's just something you're doing to keep me from asking more questions. But I'm not scared of you or your crappy attitude and I'm going to keep asking questions, so you might as well spill. What's up with you lately?"

He considered that for a moment, then drew a deep breath. "I don't think I'm going to go to school in January, either. I might take the whole year off."

I understood why he'd deferred one semester. But I was *not* expecting him to say he was planning on postponing college even more. What was this, a quarter-life crisis?

"I don't know what I want to major in, what I want to do with my life," he said.

I sat up straight, glad he was finally talking about it and maybe open to advice. "Well, what are you good at? What do you like?"

"The only thing I seem to be good at is mediumship. But isn't four years of college a whole lot of wasted time and money if I'm just going to end up back here doing what I'm already doing now?" He sighed. "Maybe I should skip college altogether."

Whoa, whoa, whoa. This was not going in the direction I'd wanted. "Perry, you don't have to have it all figured out now. Take a bunch of classes, see what strikes a chord."

He frowned. "I don't know. Look at Nate. He's known for years that he wants to be a journalist. He wrote for the school paper, got a great summer internship at the local paper, and how he's majoring in journalism. He won't just get a great job out of college. He'll get a career. He's got it all figured out."

"Not everyone does, though. If you'd gone this semester, I'm sure you'd have found that most people are like you, not Nate. And just because he knows what he wants careerwise, that doesn't mean he has everything all figured out."

"What do you mean?"

I shrugged. "I think he's pretty miserable at school."

"What gives you that idea?"

"Well, for one, he comes home to see your fug face every weekend instead of staying there."

Perry chuckled. "Yeah, *I'm* the one he comes home to see. Right."

Before I could ask what that meant, the front door slammed.

"That's either Mom or Nate," Perry whispered. "And I

don't want to talk about this college thing with either of them yet." He aimed a thumb at the door. "Make yourself scarce, little sis."

I gave him the evil eye on my way out. He couldn't hide this forever.

And Mom was not going to be happy when she found out.

THIRTEEN

GABRIEL OFFERED ME A RIDE TO SCHOOL AGAIN Monday morning, and that might have been the reason I wore my tight, nice-ass jeans rather than the slightly baggy comfortable ones I preferred. When I heard the car pull into the driveway, I gave my mom a peck on the cheek, slung my backpack over my shoulder, and headed out.

Gabriel smiled as I climbed into the passenger side. "Happy Monday."

"Yeah," I replied dumbly. I wished I had something cooler to say, like those girls who always had sexy comebacks to every statement a hot guy made. But my mind was blank, my mouth was dry, and my heart was racing.

Gabriel did that to me.

He put the car in reverse, the side of his hand grazing my thigh as he slid the gear back, then forward again into drive. My leg involuntarily jolted at his touch.

Gabriel smirked. "Do I make you nervous?"

I crossed my arms. "Of course not."

"I think I do."

"I think you flatter yourself."

He laughed then, and turned his attention back to the road. A small smile crept onto my face. It was fun and exciting being so undeniably attracted to him. I just wished he didn't know the effect he had on me.

"Any progress with the Sierra thing?" he asked as he drove.

I sighed. "No. Her mother never called to set up that reading of Sierra's room. She thinks we're frauds." I twisted the strap of my bag in frustration. "I really want to help. But there's no way for me to get my hands on Sierra's stuff without her mother's permission."

"There is one other way." Gabriel slid me a playful look.

"I am not going to break into her house!" I scoffed.

He laughed. "That's not what I was suggesting. All I'm saying is that some of her stuff isn't *in* her house anymore. The note she wrote is at the police station."

My eyes widened. "Would you get it for me?"

He gave a quick shake of his head. "There's no way my dad would let me take evidence out. But maybe he'd let me bring you in and give you a minute with it."

"Let's do it this afternoon." Hell, I'd skip school and do it now if I thought Gabriel would agree.

"I can't this afternoon. But I can do it tomorrow after school."

"Great!" I rubbed my hands together.

"I also wanted to let you know we won't be able to have these little morning drives together anymore."

My thrill at having a plan of action wavered as worry picked at the edges. "Why not?"

"I'm going to have hockey practice in the mornings, starting tomorrow. I made the team."

I exhaled loudly. Perhaps too loudly. "Oh, that's awesome! Congratulations. You're really fitting in here, making Eastport your home."

"Yeah." He had a hitch in his voice that made me turn to look at him.

"You miss it, don't you?" I asked curiously.

"Miss what?" he asked.

"New York. All the people, the places, so much to do, the hustle, the bustle. It must be so different being in a small town."

"I miss some of it. Certain friends. My family being together. The way things used to be." He paused for a moment before speaking again. "But even if I was back home, those things wouldn't be the same anyway."

I looked down at my clasped hands. "It must be hard."

"Sometimes. But there are great things about here. I can drive places, for one. The beach is beautiful. And there are certain people I'm quite fond of."

He nudged me with his shoulder. I could've melted right into the seat.

I wondered if all this reflection was brought about by his mother, but didn't want to bring it up just in case she still hadn't made contact. I'd promised her I'd let her do it her own way.

"Do you talk to your mother often?" I asked instead.

"I actually just saw her yesterday. She's in town."

"Oh?" I said innocently.

He glanced at me with a sly smile as he pulled into a front-row spot in the parking lot. "You can give up the act. She told me what you did."

I felt my face turn a fiery red. "What did she say?"

He killed the engine and chuckled. "Calm down. She was pretty impressed with you. Charging her like that, demanding to know if she was following me." He looked me over with his smoldering dark eyes. "You're small, but you're tough." He leaned toward me and whispered into my hair, "I like that."

My neck felt hot as the blushing spread. Gabriel's lips left my hair as he pulled back only a few inches from my face, never breaking eye contact. My lungs forgot how to breathe. I gripped my backpack with slippery palms.

And panicked.

I thanked him for the ride and muttered something about having to hurry. But I'm sure he knew why I made my quick exit. He knew what he did to me.

I sped past the gym and took a quick right into the main hallway, nearly steamrolling Justin in the process.

"Whoa, where's the fire?" he asked, grabbing my shoulders to steady me.

"Sorry," I said, even more discombobulated now with Justin's hands on me.

"No worries. You can crash into me anytime."

He let me go and I adjusted my backpack, glad my breathing was starting to return to normal.

"So," he said. "I need to know the color."

From the look on his face, I knew he was about to start one of his flirty games. I put my hand on my hip. "What color?"

"Of the dress you're going to wear to homecoming," he said with a confident grin. "So I know what corsage to pick out. Also, I'm wondering if I should book a limo. But we don't need to decide that today."

I was about to retort, but he gave me a playful little wave and walked on before I could. So instead I stood there like a dumbass in the middle of the hallway, my thoughts swarming around my head as students streamed by. Eventually, someone bumped into me, waking me from my coma, and I started walking again.

I climbed the stairs to the second floor, the home of my locker. I spied Cody approaching from the opposite direction.

"Slut," he muttered as he slithered by.

Normally, I let Cody's insults slide right off, and this one was laughable since I was the complete opposite of what he'd suggested. But, for some reason, it sparked an immediate rage inside me.

I stopped and yelled, "How about you sprout a thought of your own now and then instead of thinking whatever Tiffany tells you to think?"

His face contorted in anger. Maybe because I talked back instead of silently taking his abuse. Or maybe because my comment hit a nerve.

He grabbed his crotch lewdly. "I've got two crystal balls for you right here, psychic freak."

"Way to keep it classy, Cody," Mallory said, swooping in and leading me away by the arm before I could bury my fist in his face. Not that I would, but fantasizing about it for a moment was nice.

"Ignore that idiot," Mallory said.

"I usually do," I replied, taking a moment to appreciate Mallory's outfit. She wore a black skirt and purple leggings that matched her tight purple-and-pink striped shirt. I liked the style, though I always dressed as boring as possible. My motto being that there was no need to attract any further negative attention than I already got.

We finally arrived at our lockers, but the drama wasn't over. I saw it from a few feet away. Something sticking out of my locker vent. I groaned. What now?

With Mallory beside me, I plucked the object out and turned it over. It was a black-and-white photograph, a good shot. Definitely not done with a cell phone or a cheap camera. Whoever took the photo knew what they were doing and got a great close-up.

Of me. At night in my front yard, a mallet in my hand, looking around, fear evident in my eyes. It was the night I'd put up the Halloween decorations.

Someone *had* been out there.

And that person had taken a picture of me.

I looked at the back of the photo, but it was blank. The message was loud and clear, though. He could get close to me.

Mallory peered over my shoulder. "I think your secret admirer just became a secret stalker."

FOURTEEN

THE LITTLE HAIRS ON THE BACK OF MY NECK
prickled. This wasn't flattering anymore. This had become
something else. Something twisted. I felt nauseous.

I was suddenly reminded of something Madame Maslov,
the psychic I'd gotten to know over the summer, had said to
me before she left town. She'd said that I should be wary.
Because someone's love for me did not come from affection,
but from sickness.

I shoved the picture in my locker and slammed the
door shut.

"Are you all right?" Mallory put a light hand on my
shoulder.

I shook my head no. "You go on to class without me. I
need a few minutes alone."

The hallway was nearly cleared out. Mallory took one last
glance at me and then hurried into homeroom.

The bell rang as I shambled toward the bathroom, but I
didn't care about being late. I burst in and let the door close
behind me.

"You look like you're going to barf," a snarky voice echoed.

I lifted my eyes from the dirty floor. Tiffany stood at the mirror, applying lip gloss, her mouth open in a giant O.

I ignored her and headed for a stall, thinking she might be right, as nausea built in my stomach.

"What was it? Something bad?"

I stopped and turned to face her. "What are you talking about?"

"That thing sticking out of your locker. It was something disturbing, right? That's why you're hiding in here, looking all green and pukey."

Realization dawned. "You did it." I should have known. This was revenge for the cockroach in her locker, even though I wasn't the one who did that. All at once, I was relieved.

And just as quickly that relief was snatched away.

Tiffany cackled. "No, not me. But I saw who did."

I raised an eyebrow. "Yeah? Who?"

She slipped her gloss into her bag and smacked her lips together. Giving herself one last appreciative look in the mirror, she turned to leave, calling out over her shoulder, "Do your psychic mumbo jumbo and find out."

She couldn't just tell me. No, that would be too easy. Even though she was obviously taking delight in what she had seen. Or maybe she saw nothing and was just messing with me. I never knew with Tiffany.

I dropped my backpack on the floor, not caring how grimy it was down there, and gripped the sink with both hands. I needed to calm down. Even if I ran back to my locker now,

I wouldn't be able to clear my head enough to focus on the photograph.

I felt something building. Everything was smashing together and piling on top of each other, almost up to the surface, like a volcano ready to blow. Justin and Gabriel. Sierra. Friends and trust. Perry and his changes for the worse.

But I also felt something else. Something external. Something I couldn't control. And it, too, was building to a crescendo. Call it intuition, call it what you want. But that feeling scared me more than the others.

I cupped water in my hands and splashed it on my face, almost violently. The cold shocked my system, and I took deep breaths while beads of water dripped into the sink. Then I straightened and dried my skin with a paper towel. The reflection in the mirror looked better than it had a few minutes ago. Color returned to my face. Strength returned to my nerves.

I nodded and picked up my backpack. Time to see if I could get some answers.

The hallway was empty. The only sounds were the click-clack of my shoes and the muffled voice of the principal reading the morning announcements over the loudspeaker from behind the classrooms' closed doors. I dialed the combination and swung my locker door open.

The picture was right where I'd left it, slightly crinkled from the way I'd shoved it in. I smoothed it out against the wall and stared, seeing it clearly for the first time. The person obviously had a good camera. It looked like one of those professional shots. I was perfectly in focus, while the trees and

Halloween decorations behind me were blurred. The way the photo had been taken, it wasn't like the person felt menace toward his subject — me — but instead . . . appreciation.

But, still. If this boy liked me from afar, that was one thing. But to hide in the darkness, snap the photo, and then leave it here for me to find . . . that was creepy. A plan formulated in my mind. I was going to, as Tiffany so helpfully suggested, do my psychic mumbo jumbo. If it worked this time, I'd find out who this boy was. Then he and I would have a little talk about manners, social norms, and what are and aren't appropriate ways to express your feelings for a girl you're crushing on.

I closed my eyes and breathed, deep and slow. I focused on the photo, my fingers sliding across the glossy paper.

And then I saw it in my mind's eye. The photograph, in hands that were not mine. Someone was holding it, fingers slightly trembling, feeling a bit nervous. Then the person began to hook the photo into my locker vent, the blank side facing up, like how I found it.

I started to panic, not wanting to lose the image before I could find out who it was. But my visions were from the point of view of the other person. I needed him to catch a reflection of himself in a mirror. Or for someone to walk by and call out his name.

Come on, I thought. *Before it's gone.*

But then something did pique my interest. He had a silver ring on the thumb of his right hand. A hand that was decidedly not masculine after all.

A girl was doing this to me?

The photo was now lodged in place, but before the girl let go, she looked down. I caught a quick glimpse of bright purple leggings.

I jerked back in surprise, my eyes snapping open, the vision gone.

It was Mallory.

My stalker was Mallory.

FIFTEEN

I AVOIDED EVERYONE THE REST OF THE DAY. THE next morning, Mallory tried to talk to me at our lockers, but she must have seen the fire in my eyes when I glared at her. She backed away and kept her distance until the end of the school day.

I wandered outside, waiting for Gabriel. We were supposed to meet to go to the police station. I hoped he hadn't forgotten. I was about to pull out my phone and call him when someone started yelling.

A little shouting in the parking lot wasn't all that unusual. But this person wasn't playing. That voice was mad. Spitting mad.

I peered around a giant SUV and saw Cody pacing back and forth by his truck. His arms flailed in the air, and a stream of expletives poured from his mouth. A small group of people had formed around him, all shaking their heads in what looked like mock sympathy.

"He is so pissed," Kendra said, strutting up to me. "He loves that truck."

"What happened?" I asked.

"Someone keyed the side and flattened his tire."

"Oh." I tried to drum up some empathy. I'd been in the victim position enough to understand. But I couldn't manage to feel anything for Cody.

I was reminded of the cockroach in Tiffany's locker, and a tiny smile crept onto my face. Cody had been bullying kids like me since preschool. I wasn't about to feel sorry for him when he got a little taste of it.

"Can I talk to you?" someone asked.

I pulled my eyes from Cody's meltdown. Mallory stood beside me, waiting for an answer, her eyes a bit glassy. Kendra flipped her hair over her shoulder and rushed off, as if unpopularity were contagious.

"What do you want?" I said, my voice flat.

With Kendra gone, Mallory moved closer to me. "I just want to know what I did wrong. Why you hate me all of a sudden. You're acting just like . . ."

Her voice trailed off, but I figured she was about to insert the name of one of the blondes.

"I know it was you, all right?" I snapped.

Mallory blinked rapidly. "Me what?"

"You're the one who's been sending me notes. You took the picture of me and stuck it in my locker."

"What?" Her face was pained. "Why would you think that?"

I put my hand up. "Don't even bother lying. I saw it. Okay? Saw. It." I pointed to my head so she'd understand I got a vision.

"No. It wasn't me. The photograph, yeah, I held it. But I wasn't the one who took the picture."

"Su-ure." I turned to walk away, but she grabbed the sleeve of my jacket.

"I found it on the floor. It must have been stuck in the vent of your locker and fell. So I picked it up, realized what it was, and stuck it back in the vent."

Her eyes were wild, desperate for me to believe her.

"Why wouldn't you just tell me, instead of pretending you hadn't seen it before?" I asked.

"I figured you'd think it was me who took it. It was obviously taken when you were alone in your yard, right before I showed up. You know I'm interested in photography."

She didn't look like someone who was lying. And her story didn't contradict my vision in any way. But still . . . I shook my head.

"This!" She pointed at me and raised her voice, catching the attention of a couple kids walking by. "What you're doing right now . . . is why I didn't tell you. I knew you'd suspect me. I knew better than to trust you. And I was right."

Those words hurt. I didn't want to be one of those judgy people. Like the kids who called me freak without even getting to know me.

Mallory started walking away, head down.

"I want to believe you aren't the person who's been messing with me," I called out.

She stopped and turned. "Just . . . do the same thing to the other notes, then. You'll see it wasn't me."

"I have."

"And what did you get?"

"Nothing."

"So." She crossed her arms and jutted her chin out. "Your line of thought is that I went out of my way to wear gloves or something so you wouldn't get a vision from my creepy notes, but then I just bare handled the photograph? Come on. I'm not that dumb."

She was right. It made no sense. Whoever left the first two notes knew about my gift and did something to hide their imprint. They'd obviously do the same with the picture. But it fell from the locker vent to the floor, and Mallory had the bad luck to pick it up.

I'd treated her like dirt for something she didn't do. And the reason she wasn't honest with me from the start was because she knew I'd act this way.

I looked up, ready to apologize, but she was gone. I reared my foot back and kicked at a rock on the ground, watching it skitter across the pavement. It didn't make me feel better.

"What did that poor pebble ever do to you?" Gabriel swaggered over. His bag was slung over one shoulder. Normally just the sight of him in his black fleece and low-slung jeans would be enough to turn my day around, but it wasn't working.

"Bad day," I explained.

He tilted his head to the side. "Maybe some detective work will help."

I sat in a chair in the police station's reception area and stared at the discolored linoleum floor. Gabriel had gone through the large metal door and down the hall to his father's desk.

And now I waited to see if he could convince Detective Toscano to let me have a minute with Sierra's note.

Other than the dispatcher, who doubles as the receptionist, I was the only one in the room. During the summer the building was busier, the station bustling with seasonal officers the town added to deal with the influx of tourists. But this time of year, things were relatively quiet. I spent a minute or two staring down the artificial plant in the corner. For the season, it was adorned with a fake spiderweb, spread from leaf to leaf. A giant decorative spider sat in the middle, smiling with its fangs.

A hand landed on my shoulder.

I startled and looked up into Phil Tisdell's worried face.

Phil was a fellow townie about my mom's age, and a really nice guy. He'd been crushing on my mom for years. I pitied him. Mom flirted with him enough to keep him hanging on, even though she never dated anyone. I think she was still waiting for Dad to walk through the front door.

"Is everything all right, Clare? Why are you here?" Phil asked.

"I'm fine, Phil," I said. "I'm here with a friend."

"Oh." His hand lay over his heart.

I realized how it must have looked, me sitting in the station waiting room, a somber look on my face. "You working today?" I asked. The town hall, where Phil worked, was housed in the same building.

"Yeah, yeah," he said, loosening up. "I came down here for some paperwork."

"Okay." I smiled. "I'll let you get back to it."

He gave a little wave and started to walk away, but then stopped. "Uh, Clare?"

"Yes, Phil?"

He shuffled his feet back and forth. "I was thinking of asking your mother to accompany me to my sister's wedding next month. Do you think that's a good idea?"

Oh, poor lovesick Phil. "I think that's a great idea." His face started to light up before I added, "But I don't know if she'll say yes. You know how she is."

His whole body seemed to sag.

"It's worth asking, though, right?" I said cheerily.

"Sure, sure," he mumbled. He walked away as Gabriel strode up to me.

"What was that about?" he asked, eyeing Phil.

"He's in love with my mother."

"Uh, okay. You ready?"

"As I'll ever be."

I followed him down the hall and into the station's one and only interrogation room.

"Dad's bringing it in here," Gabriel explained.

A moment later, Detective Toscano walked in, looking a little worse for wear. I wondered why he was so tired. It wasn't like they were working around the clock on the Sierra Waldman case.

Then I remembered. Mrs. Toscano was back in town. And that was obviously having an effect on Gabriel's dad.

The note was in a clear baggy. He placed it on the table

and said, "The mother confirmed this is her daughter's hand-writing. We're probably going to return it soon since there is no case at present."

"I came at the right time, then," I said, feeling slightly uncomfortable, knowing Detective Toscano's true feelings about psychics.

We all paused a moment and I shot a quick look at Gabriel. I really didn't want his dad here, watching over my shoulder. That might mess with my mojo.

Gabriel caught on. "Can we have a minute, Dad?"

He blinked quickly. "Of course. I'll come back." He backed out of the room and closed the door.

I let out a long breath, hoping my unease would go with it. Gabriel and I sat on opposite sides of the table. He nudged the bag toward me with a finger. "Whenever you're ready."

I slid the note out and grasped it with both hands. I closed my eyes and took several deep breaths through my nose. Even with the door closed, I could hear the sounds of the station — the phone ringing, loud conversations, a boisterous laugh. But after a few moments, I felt that familiar buzzing in my body, and the interrogation room faded into the background while a different room appeared before my closed eyes.

She was holding a pen in her right hand and keeping the paper still with the palm of her left. She wrote each word slowly, in large looping letters. I could feel her excitement, but also some anxiety. She was wondering if she was making the right choice.

I felt a hand on her shoulder, urging her on.

She finished the note and folded it up.

"So I'll leave this for my mom, grab some stuff, and come back." It sounded like a question.

I was hoping the person Sierra was with would reply before she stuffed the note in her bag. I pleaded with the vision, with Sierra, to hold on to the paper a bit longer.

But she didn't.

All I got before the vision was lost was a quick glance up . . . at a desk. A dark, perhaps cherry wood desk. Plain, with no pictures or anything else on it. Very unlike that of a teenage girl.

SIXTEEN

I WAS DISAPPOINTED WITH WHAT LITTLE I GOT from the vision. Gabriel said it was a big accomplishment, though. I'd reaffirmed that Sierra had written the note and obviously voluntarily run away. She was a legal adult. Therefore, no case. But still . . . something inside me wouldn't settle. Wouldn't accept that. Maybe it was that layer of anxiety I'd felt under Sierra's excitement when she wrote the note.

Wednesday after school, I tried to lose myself in homework. I finished all my assignments and caught up on my reading, but still felt tense. I looked up the Waldmans' phone number and dialed quickly while I still had the nerve.

It rang several times and eventually went to voice mail.

I cleared my throat. "Hi, Mrs. Waldman? This is Clare Fern. I just wanted to let you know that, um, if you're still interested, I would love to help out any way I can. I could come and try reading Sierra's room. If you'd like. Okay. Thanks. Bye."

Ugh, I was awful at leaving messages.

I hung up, doubting she'd call me back. She probably still thought we were useless frauds. But I felt a little bit better after reaching out. At least I was trying.

I groaned and went downstairs for a soda and chocolate fix. I also hoped Mom would be around, since I wanted to go for a drive.

Mom was at the kitchen table, surrounded by bubble mailers, working on some project of hers. I watched her from the doorway. She was always home, working, supporting her family. She never went out with friends or dated or did anything wild and crazy. Her thoughts were always on Perry and me, never on herself.

There's a story Mom likes to tell about one time when I was three. She was organizing photographs, and I found one of her as a teenager, at an amusement park with friends. I stared at the picture and asked, "Who was babysitting me and Perry?" When Mom explained that I hadn't been born yet, I'd had the realization, for the first time, that Mom had lived a long life before me. Without me. It was startling for a three-year-old.

Even now, it sometimes seems strange to think about. Mom, Perry, and I were like the Three Musketeers. We fought, sure, but always remained close-knit. Always loved and lived for one another. Things were changing, though. Perry would be, hopefully, shipping off to college soon. And I would, too, in a couple of years. And Mom would stay here, alone.

For most of my childhood, I was delighted that Mom never remarried or even dated. First, because of my fantasy that Dad would return to re-sweep her off her feet. But also because I was selfish. Mom lavished attention on Perry and me. I hadn't wanted some random man to come in and take that away. To steal my time with her.

But now I chided myself for those old selfish feelings. My mother was a telepath. Of course she'd heard me thinking those thoughts once or twice when I was younger. And she'd sacrificed her own happiness for my aversion to change.

Now, as I watched her at the kitchen table, I worried about what would happen in two years. Because if Mom was left here, sad and lonely, it would be my fault.

Mom noticed me in the doorway and smiled. "Would you look at this?" She gestured to the chaos on the table.

"What is all that?" I said, walking to the fridge and grabbing a Diet Coke.

"Orders, my dear. Tons of orders."

"For those ugly muumuus you made?"

Mom closed her eyes and exhaled through her nose. "They are called tapestry dresses, and they're obviously not ugly since I sold each one I put up on eBay."

"Really? Congratulations." I cracked open the soda and took a gulp.

Mom narrowed her eyes at me.

"What?"

She tapped her fingers on the table. "I'm waiting for your compulsory sarcastic remark."

I laughed. "Seriously, Mom. Congratulations. I think it's cool. You always said you wanted to start a little side business selling those things you make."

She beamed. "Thank you, Clarity."

"I still wouldn't wear one if you paid me, though."

Mom pinched the bridge of her nose. "Don't you have homework to do? Boys to pine over?"

"Actually, I was hoping you'd take me out driving. My learner's permit is getting dusty."

"I can't right now." She patted the chair next to her. "Chat with me for a minute while I organize these orders. Do you see a pink dress anywhere?"

I sat beside her and riffled through a stack of neatly folded dresses. I held one up. "Is this it?"

"Yes, thank you." She took it from me and then began searching for something else. "So what's new in your life, honey?"

Mom wasn't exactly gung ho over my desire to help the Waldmans. And since my trip to the station had resulted in a big nothing, I didn't feel the need to go into it. I was even more reluctant to tell her about the secret admirer. She'd just flip out and put me under house arrest. And there was no reason for it. The person was creepy, but it's not like he'd threatened to kill me or anything. And Mom would completely overreact and make my life a living hell.

"Nothing much," I lied.

"I like that girl Mallory, who came over to help you with the Halloween decorations."

I frowned. "How could you like her? You didn't even meet her." Then I realized what she'd done. "Oh, Mom."

She shrugged. "I heard you outside talking to someone. You seemed a little nervous at first, so I listened in a bit. It was harmless."

"Mom, you can't do that to every friend who comes over."

"She was a stranger, talking to my daughter outside at night," she said indignantly. "I could either go outside, introduce myself, and embarrass you, or peer out the window and listen in to her thoughts for a minute."

"In that case, thanks, I guess."

"She's a nice girl. She likes you." Mom paused. "A lot."

"That's great, Mom," I said unenthusiastically.

Her tongue stuck out of the side of her mouth as she concentrated on peeling an address label off the backing. "I would really like for you to put yourself out there more. Go do normal teenager stuff. Especially during the school year when we're not busy at home. I know you've been invited to things this year and haven't gone."

I watched a drop of water trickle down the side of the soda can. "Those girls at school aren't real friends. They're just interested in what I can do."

"But if you'd let them get to know you instead of keeping them at arm's length, then I'm sure they'd come to love all of you."

"I don't care if they like me or not. They called me freak girl for years."

"And I heard you call them the Barbie Brigade," Mom retorted.

"I say that to Perry, not to their faces."

"Is it really that much better?" She added the finished mailer to a pile on the floor. "They judged you, you judge them. Maybe it's time to put an end to all that. They're reaching out to you, Clare. Why not give it a try?"

A slow smile spread across my lips as an idea occurred to me. "I'll make a deal with you. The next time the Barbie Brigade invites me to something, I'll say yes."

"Under what condition?" Mom asked suspiciously.

"The next time Phil Tisdell asks you out, you say yes. You give *that* a try."

She sighed heavily and clasped her hands.

"Perry and I both want you to be happy, Mom." I added in a soft voice. "No one would blame you for moving on."

"Just one date?" she asked.

"That's the deal."

"Fine."

"Yes!" I pumped my arm for this small yet giant victory. I pushed back my chair and stood up, stretching. "Now let's take a break so you can teach me how to parallel park."

She looked down at all the work she hadn't finished. "I really don't have the time, honey."

"But I need the practice. My test is next month."

"Periwinkle!" Mom's yell echoed off the kitchen walls.

I winced. "Warn me the next time you're going to do that."

Perry trotted in a moment later. "Yeah?"

Mom, carefully wrapping a dress in tissue paper, said, "Could you take your sister out for a while? Let her practice driving?"

His eyes widened. "No, I'm too busy."

"Doing what?" I asked.

"Um, I have to, ah, build Mom a new website to sell her dresses on. So she doesn't have to go through eBay."

Mom raised an eyebrow. "You said you couldn't get started on that until I tell you what URL I want to purchase."

"Well, yeah, but I was starting to, ah, conceptualize . . ."

Mom tilted her head slightly while Perry um'd and ah'd. He didn't notice, but I knew she was taking a listen.

Finally, she slapped her hand on the table. "Stop this nonsense. You're helping your sister and that's that."

His face darkened. "Fine." He swiveled on his foot and stomped out of the kitchen.

Mom called out, "You'll appreciate it after she has her license and doesn't bug you to chauffeur her around anymore."

I gave her a dirty look and whispered, "You listened to his thoughts."

She shrugged. "I wanted to see what his problem was. He won't tell me. I had no other choice. I had to make sure he was all right."

"And?"

She waved her hand theatrically in the air. "He's just being lazy. He was only thinking, 'I don't wanna go out. I don't wanna go out.' Over and over. Whining like a baby. I don't know what to do about him."

If she only knew what I knew: that Perry was considering skipping college altogether. She'd have a conniption.

I swiped Perry's car keys off the hook and bolted past him on our way out. I scooted in behind the wheel, excitement pumping through my veins. Driving gave me a rush, a small taste of the freedom to come.

Perry cast one last wistful look at the house, then got in the passenger side.

"Oh, wipe the doom and gloom off your face," I said. "It won't be that bad."

He grunted in response.

"I was thinking we could go down Hickory Lane."

"Sure," Perry muttered.

I took care backing out of the driveway, since we live on a main road. It would have been more difficult during the summer months, but now it took only a few moments for me to see the road was clear. I backed out, then shifted into drive. I pressed the accelerator too hard at first, then let up completely and the car jerked. I cringed, waiting for Perry to snap at me, but he stayed silent.

I kept the speed steady the rest of the way down Rigsdale and was starting to feel a bit proud of myself.

"You're hugging the curb," Perry said through gritted teeth.

"Sorry." I saw that he was right. I was a bit nervous about the oncoming traffic and overcompensated by steering too close to the sidewalk instead of the dotted line. I corrected it.

"Thanks for the tip," I added, wanting Perry to know I appreciated his taking me out like this. "Hey, I got Mom to agree to go on a date with Phil."

I was expecting some form of "how the hell did you accomplish that?" but Perry only said, "That's great."

I risked a glance at him. He looked pale, almost sick, with beads of sweat gathering on his forehead. He gripped the door handle so hard, you'd think I was going a hundred miles an hour. I checked the speedometer, just in case. I was only going thirty. What was his problem?

I was so weirded out by his behavior that I didn't see the light had turned red until we were almost upon it. I had to slam on the brakes.

Perry braced himself against the dashboard with both hands. "Clare! Red means stop, you know."

"I know. I'm sorry."

The light turned green and I took a right onto quiet Hickory Lane, sometimes called Cottage Row by locals. It was a long road ending in a cul-de-sac, filled with cute little cottages. They were almost all vacation homes or summer rentals, now dark and empty in the fall. I let out a deep breath, feeling more comfortable.

"We should turn back," Perry said, his voice catching.

"Don't worry. This road is empty. I can't run any-one over."

"I've had enough." His voice shook. "Let's go home."

I looked over at him and was startled. He'd seemed ner-vous before, but now he was terrified. His chest heaved in and out with each breath. Sweat stained his T-shirt. His hands were balled into bright white fists on his lap.

"What's the matter with you?" I asked. "Are you sick?"

"Watch out!" he yelled, reaching for the wheel.

I turned back to the road just in time to see that while I was looking aghast at my brother, the car had swerved to the right. Directly at a man dragging a trash can down his drive-way. A look of terror flashed on the man's face as he flung himself backward. I jerked the wheel to the left, but Perry had reached out for it at the same time and accidentally pulled it to the right. I slammed on the brakes. The car fishtailed. And finally it stalled, after hitting something with a sickening crunch.

SEVENTEEN

I OPENED MY EYES. IT TOOK A FEW SECONDS TO focus because I'd squeezed them shut so hard at the moment of impact. My hands still gripped the wheel, my arms stick-straight. I took a quick mental inventory to see if I was hurt, but I didn't feel anything.

I brought my hands down to my lap in slow motion and turned to Perry. His eyes were open, but he looked like he was about to vomit. He brought his hands up to his face and pressed on his forehead.

"Are you okay?" I asked.

He nodded quickly. "Let's go."

"We can't go. I hit something."

He ignored me and doubled over in his seat, face still covered.

My legs felt stiff as I got out and walked around to the back of the car, terrified of what I might find. A pickup truck sat in the driveway, its tailgate down. A rubber trash can lay on its side, but I didn't think that was what I hit.

"What happened?" an angry voice asked.

I whirled around and saw a man getting up from the grass, wiping his pants off.

"I'm so sorry," I pleaded as I rushed over to him. "I wasn't paying attention. My brother looked sick and I was staring at him and the car swerved —"

I stopped as I recognized the man I'd just nearly killed. "Mr. Rylander?"

His mouth, too, opened in the surprise of recognition. "Clare Fern?" He frowned. "This kind of high jinks is the last thing I expected from someone like you." He stepped closer and sniffed. "Have you been drinking?"

A teacher. I nearly ran over one of my teachers. I wished I could turn invisible. I glanced over my shoulder. Perry was still in the car, probably spraying puke all over the place, thanks to whatever bug he had. I turned back, my long hair covering half my face as I stared at the ground.

"I wasn't drinking. I'm just apparently a bad driver. I'm very sorry." Then I remembered the crunch. I gaped at him. "Did I hit you?"

"No, I launched myself backward just in time. You did, however, smash my fence."

I walked over to my back bumper and there it was. One panel of a cute white picket fence on the ground under my tire. My hand flew up to my mouth. "I'm so sorry!"

"As you've said." Rylander crossed his arms.

I was relieved that I hadn't hit him, but also nervous. I had no idea how much it cost to fix a fence, but however much it was, it was probably more than I had at the moment. I rubbed the back of my neck. "I'll, um, call my mother, and . . ."

"Don't worry about it," he said, dropping his arms.

"What?"

"I don't want to get you in trouble. I'm pretty handy with stuff like this. I'll have that fence fixed in no time."

"Really?" Gratitude washed over me. For once, I was glad Rylander tried so hard to be Mr. Likable. If it was Mr. Frederick, I'd have been in handcuffs.

"You should take him to a doctor, though." He pointed at the car, where Perry was hunched over.

"I will," I said, nodding gratefully. "I'll get him checked out right away."

I slid back into the driver's seat, then wondered if that was such a great idea. After all, my driving practice had just ended in a fail with a capital F.

"You should probably drive," I said to my brother.

Perry shook his head vehemently. "Just go. Go now." He covered his ears with his hands, like he was trying to block out my voice. But I wasn't even talking.

"I think I should take you to the ER."

He turned to me, his face distorted into something I didn't recognize. "Take. Me. Home. Now!"

"Okay, okay." I turned the ignition and the car started. Thankfully, it was all in one piece. The bumper was damaged, but it could have been a lot worse.

I felt a little bump as the back tires came down off the curb. I was paranoid now and kept the speed at twenty, my eyes staring straight ahead.

"Just stop!" Perry yelled. "I can't listen right now!" He pulled his head down between his knees.

"I'm not talking," I said, taking a peek at him. He was in the crash position and I wondered if he had hit his head after all. But I didn't want a repeat of what had just happened, so I forced my eyes to stay on the road this time, ignoring his moaning and groaning.

When we were almost home, he brought his head up, leaned back, and started to take deep breaths. As soon as I pulled into the driveway, he bolted out of the car, leaving the door open. I closed both doors and looked up at the house with my jaw clenched. Perry had run inside. He was probably already blabbing to Mom about what I did.

I lumbered up the porch and gingerly shut the door behind me, hoping to sneak upstairs.

"Clare?" Mom called out.

My shoulders slumped. "Coming." I walked into the kitchen like a prisoner to execution.

Mom was stacking up her packages. "I'm heading out to the post office to mail these. How did the driving go?"

My eyes darted back and forth. "Where's Perry?"

She shrugged. "Back to his room, I suppose. He bolted up the stairs without a word."

He didn't tattle, which was nice, but Mom was sure to see the giant dent in the bumper when she went out to the driveway.

"It didn't exactly go smoothly," I admitted.

With a worried look, Mom unloaded the packages from her arms back onto the table. "What happened?"

"Perry looked really sick. I thought he was going to throw up. And I was watching him instead of the road and . . . long story short, there's a dent in the back bumper."

Mom's hand flew up to her chest. "Did you hit another car?"

"No, a fence. But it's fine. Everything's fine. No thanks to Perry."

"It's sounds like you're trying to blame your brother for your mistake," she said, furrowing her brow.

"I'm not. I mean, if he wasn't acting psychotic, I would have had my eyes on the road, but yeah, I know it's my fault. I'll pay Perry for the repair somehow."

Mom let out a long exhale. "Perry's not fixing that old beast. It probably has less than a year of life left in it. It can still run with a dent in the bumper." She shook her finger at me. "But from now on, you're only doing your driving with me."

I never wanted to get in a car with Perry again, so that was fine. I helped Mom load the packages into her car. After she drove away, I inspected the damage to Perry's bumper. It really wasn't that bad, but I still didn't truly understand what had happened. Perry had been on edge as soon as we left the house. It got increasingly worse the farther away we got. Then, after the accident, it was like he was a crazy person. What had happened in that car?

I looked slyly at the passenger side. I *could* try to find out.

I glanced up at the house windows to make sure Perry wasn't watching, then jumped into the passenger seat.

When we first started out, he'd been gripping the door handle, so I gripped it tightly with my right hand. I closed my eyes and tried to concentrate.

The image flickered around the edges for a moment and then came into full view. Perry's eyes were on the road, nowhere else. He never looked at me. Never looked out the window. Just straight ahead. I heard myself chattering to him, but tried to tune that out and focus on Perry's inner thoughts.

Oh man, I don't feel good.

It's happening again.

I should have found a way to stay home.

Okay, try to stay calm. Take deep breaths. That website said you can talk yourself through this. Ugh. How can I talk myself through a heart attack?!

Then the car stopped short and the vision ended. That must have been when I slammed on the brakes at the light. I thought back to where Perry's hands went then: the dashboard.

I placed my palms on the dash, where I would if I were bracing myself. Nothing came at first, so I spaced them out a little wider. The vision came quickly. An intense flash.

"Clare! Red means stop, you know."

I heard myself apologizing, then the car took a right onto Hickory, and the vision ended. Perry must have returned his hands to his lap. I felt around a bit more: on the seat, the belt, but no visions surfaced. I was pretty sure Perry had his hands either balled up on his lap or gripping his head the rest of the way.

Two things concerned me. One, Perry had obviously been hiding a secret. He wasn't just grumpy all the time. He'd been battling anxiety. And laziness wasn't keeping him stuck in the house like a recluse. Panic attacks were.

My other concern was that I still hadn't found out what changed *after* the accident. Perry had obviously been hearing a voice. But I had no way to find out what was going on in his head on the way home because he hadn't touched anything.

I looked up at his window again. I guess I could try asking.

I went upstairs to Perry's room. It was messy, as usual. His bed was unmade. His desk was covered in papers and books. His walls hadn't changed since he was nine years old. They still had the same faded pennants: Red Sox, Bruins, Patriots, Celtics.

Perry, though, had changed.

He sat at his desk, staring down at his hands.

"Are you sure you don't want to go to the doctor?"

"I'm fine now," he said.

"What happened back there?" I asked softly.

He moved to his bed and sat down. "I didn't feel well."

"I did a reading on the passenger side," I confessed. "I know about the anxiety."

I expected him to yell at me about invading his privacy, but instead he looked relieved. "Something changed inside me after everything happened this summer. I started to have these horrible feelings when I left home. Sweating, ragged breathing, chest pain, nausea."

I sank down beside him. "Panic attacks."

"Yeah." He blinked back tears. "The first time it happened, I didn't understand. I thought I was dying. Having a heart attack or something. But as soon as I was safely back home, it stopped. It started to happen more and more, and then I was scared to leave the house because I feared the panic attack that I knew would come." He shook his head. "I know this probably makes no sense to you."

"It makes perfect sense," I said. "I saw a show about this once. You have agoraphobia." I paused. "And I'm a huge jerk. I complained when you didn't want to drive me places. When you deferred college." I raked my hands through my hair. "Why didn't I see what was really going on?"

Perry smiled sadly. "You don't get it, do you? You're the strong one, not me. Yeah, I know the right things to say to people, but there's a big difference between charisma and strength. You've got strength. That's why you didn't see it. It wouldn't even occur to you that I'd become afraid to leave the house."

I wanted to tell him he was wrong. My whole life, I'd thought of Perry as the strong one and me as the meek one. He was extroverted and charismatic. He could calm Mom down quicker than a glass of wine. But here he was, saying I had the strength in the family. Despite how much I disagreed, he didn't need me to be contrary right now.

Tears stung my eyes. I felt guilty for every time I'd snapped at him. For seeing him as moody instead of seeing someone who needed help. "I'm sorry I wasn't more supportive."

He shrugged. "You would have been if I'd just been

honest. I don't know why I didn't tell you. I was embarrassed, I guess." He stared down at the floor.

"There's nothing to be embarrassed about. We went through a lot over the summer. You wouldn't be human if you weren't affected by that."

"You weren't," he said, his eyes snapping up to mine. "You moved on. You want to go do more cases. You want to be Spider-Man."

I grinned at his joke. "People handle things in different ways. Plus, you went through a lot more than I did. I didn't even know the girl who was killed. You did. They fingered you as the killer. You were staring down a life in prison at one point. Of course you're not going to come out of that unscathed."

"I'm working hard to try to fix it," he said. "Don't tell Mom, okay? I want to try to handle this on my own."

"Okay, but first you have to tell me what happened *after* the accident. Who were you yelling at?"

He looked at me steadily. "It was that Ashley girl."

I squinted, confused. "The one who came through during Mrs. Waldman's reading?"

"Yeah. After the crash, she was there, yelling in my head. And it makes no sense. I wasn't even focused."

No wonder he'd been so shaken up. "Sometimes I'm hit with visions when I'm not concentrating," I said. "It's rare, but it happens."

He shook his head. "My gift doesn't work like that. I have to *try*. And I didn't. She just barreled through."

It was true. Perry didn't have ghosts following him around

all day. He didn't see dead people while he walked through the mall. It took a lot of effort for him to connect with a spirit. So for Ashley to bust in like that was highly unusual.

"Maybe you were so freaked out by the accident, you opened your mind without realizing." I lapsed into silence. "Who cares why it happened. What did she say? Was she any more coherent this time?"

"Hardly. Again, she was panicked, almost screaming." He brought a shaky hand to his forehead. "It hurt my head."

Perry's shoulders were slumped forward, his eyes sunken. Even voluntary readings tended to tire Perry a bit, but this one seemed to suck all the energy from him.

"Were you able to make out anything she said?"

"I got her full name. Ashley Reed. I'm not sure, but I think she said she was famous. Or 'a famous' something or other. I don't know. All I got was that and one other thing."

"It should be easy enough to figure out." I got off the bed, sat at his desk, and opened his laptop. It was already on, so I went to the search engine and typed "Ashley Reed."

Perry fell back on the bed. "Read it to me."

My eyes skimmed the listings. "There's nothing. If she was famous, there would be something on the first page. But there's nothing really." I went to pages two and three. "Just regular people named Ashley Reed with Facebook pages and stuff. No one famous." I clicked over to the news section and retried the search. "Nothing in the news under that name, either."

"Maybe I heard her wrong," Perry mumbled, rolling onto his side and curling into a ball.

I closed the laptop. "So what was the other thing?"

He opened one eye and said sleepily, "What other thing?"

"You said you only understood one other thing she said. What was it?"

"Oh." He closed his eyes again. "She said, 'It's happening again.'"

I sat and stared at my brother as his breaths came deep and slow, indicating sleep. In my mind, I replayed the words Ashley had said. And I couldn't help the feeling that her message was for me.

EIGHTEEN

THURSDAY PASSED IN A HAZE OF CLASSES, AND THAT afternoon I sat in the kitchen. I should have been doing homework, but I couldn't stop thinking about Ashley. Perry was never able to contact a spirit unless they were connected to the place we were, or the person we were with. Ashley had appeared at our house and at the accident scene, two different places. She'd appeared when we were trying to contact Sierra, but Mrs. Waldman didn't know any Ashley. The more I thought about it, the more I realized the only commonality was us. But I didn't know anyone with that name. And neither did Perry, unless he was lying.

The phone rang, so I hurried for the receiver on the kitchen wall.

"May I speak with Clare, please?" a woman's voice asked.

"This is she."

The caller cleared her throat. "This is Tracy Waldman, Sierra's mother, returning your call."

My heart beat a little faster. "Is there any news?"

"Unfortunately, no. But I would like to take you up on your offer to come to my house to see if you could pick up any clues about Sierra." Her voice cracked. "I've gotten nowhere on my own."

"Of course. When is good for you?"

"How about now?"

"Sure. I'll see you soon."

I stared at the phone in my hand for a moment, wondering how that had happened so fast. Then I hung it up, suddenly feeling a little uncomfortable with the idea of going to the Waldmans' house alone. I wouldn't put Perry through the stress, and Mom was out buying fabric. Plus, it was clear Mom wanted no part of this.

The hardwood floor creaked behind me.

I turned and startled at the sight of Justin in the kitchen doorway.

"Perry let me in," he explained with a sheepish smile.

I wasn't exactly disappointed to see him, but I didn't want him to know that and read too much into it, either. I forced a frown. "You've got to stop coming by uninvited."

"Then you've got to start inviting me over."

I tried hard to keep them straight, but the corners of my mouth lifted up. Justin leaned against the wall and crossed his arms, his head tilted to the side as he studied me. "So I heard you on the phone. Where're you going?"

I figured there wasn't any harm in telling him. "To Sierra Waldman's house. To see if I can pick up on anything."

His brow furrowed. "I thought she just ran away."

"She might've. Or not. That's what I'm trying to help her mother with."

Justin paused for a moment, as if carefully considering what he wanted to say next. "A little birdie told me that you have a secret admirer."

I wondered who this squawker was, but didn't ask. "You knew that already. You were the one who found the flowers."

"I assumed they were from Toscano."

"No, Gabriel says it's not him."

"And it's not me, so . . . who is it?"

I gave a slight shrug. "I honestly don't know. I'd like to know, because it's starting to give me the heebie-jeebies."

"Me, too. Though I'd have gone with a different word choice."

I arched an eyebrow. "So that's why you're here."

He held up one hand. "Guilty. I heard about the picture in your locker. I wanted to check on you."

I was part flattered, part annoyed. "I'm fine. I don't need a babysitter."

"I figured. It takes a lot more than a picture to scare you." He rubbed his hands together. "Okay, when are we leaving?"

"For where?"

"Sierra's. I'll drive you and come along for the fun."

I hesitated. Just minutes ago, I'd been thinking I didn't want to go alone. But Justin pulling the whole *helpless little girl needs a big strong man* act made me want to turn him down on principle.

"It's not going to be 'fun,'" I argued.

He crooked his finger at me, daring me to come closer.

I inched forward.

"What's the matter?" he said. "Afraid to be alone with me? Afraid you won't be able to resist my charm?"

I rolled my eyes and grabbed my bag. Now I had something to prove. "Let's go, Romeo."

Justin had gotten his license only a month ago, but after my fence fiasco, I didn't have the right to judge anyone's driving. So I kept my mouth shut when he ran over the curb, backing out of my driveway. He fiddled with the radio until he found the alternative rock station.

"Daddy's car doesn't have that preset?" I teased.

"Sorry I don't have my own car like *Gabriel* does." He drew out Gabriel's name mockingly. "I heard he's been driving you to school."

"Only twice," I said.

"All the girls in school are going all gaga over him. The new plaything. They're like sheep, don't you think?" His eyes slid toward mine.

I knew what he was doing. The last thing I ever wanted was to be a follower. But simple reverse psychology wouldn't work on me. My attraction to Gabriel was no more about what other people thought than my relationship with Justin was.

"Pay attention to the road, Justin."

He grinned and drummed his fingers on the steering wheel to the music. We arrived a few minutes later. The Waldmans' house was a Cape-style, almost identical to Mallory's next door. I wondered if Mallory was home. My eyes went to her upstairs window, thinking I glimpsed movement. I squinted and looked again, but saw only curtains.

I knocked on the Waldmans' door and heard feet shuffling inside. Mrs. Waldman slowly opened the door. She looked rough, with rumpled clothes and dark bags under her eyes. She didn't seem surprised that I had a friend with me. Her eyes didn't register anything but resignation.

She told me where to find Sierra's room and then returned to the chair I assumed she'd been sitting in when we arrived, facing the window, surrounded by only the sound of a grandfather clock ticking.

My shoes squeaked as I walked up the staircase. The walls of the upstairs hallway were plastered with photos of Sierra at piano recitals from about age three until twelve or so.

"There aren't any pictures of her as a teen," Justin whispered, noticing it just as I did.

It seemed that when their marriage started to fall apart, Mr. and Mrs. Waldman also forgot how to use a camera. From recent school gossip, I knew that Sierra's parents became serial daters after their divorce. Sierra was shuffled back and forth between their houses as prospective stepmothers and stepfathers were paraded in front of her and quickly forgotten.

Those years must have been quite the change for Sierra. Growing up as a homeschooled child prodigy and the center of her parents' world and then slowly losing that attention year after year until last month, when she was pushed into a school where everyone knew each other and no one had time for her, including her own parents.

I opened Sierra's door, and Justin closed it behind him. The room was small, or maybe it just seemed that way because her furniture was gigantic. A white-canopied sleigh bed was pushed up against one wall, and a nightstand, tall dresser, desk, and vanity took up all the space on the other. A pair of jeans was balled up on the unmade bed and various pairs of shoes littered the floor. Mrs. Waldman had obviously kept the room as Sierra had left it.

"Where do you want to start?" Justin looked exhilarated, like a kid on an adventure. A far cry from the last time I cased a bedroom with someone. That had been over the summer, with Gabriel the skeptic.

"According to the police," I said, taking in the surroundings, "she took her personal stuff with her. Purse, laptop, all that stuff."

"Sounds like a runaway to me," Justin said, lowering himself onto the bed.

"What are you doing?" I said in a loud whisper.

He folded his arms behind his head and leaned back. "Staying out of your way." He patted the space beside him. "Unless you'd like to join me."

I ignored him and opened the door to Sierra's closet. I was hoping to find a big box o' secrets hidden away on a top shelf under some sweaters. But there were only clothes. And more shoes. Seemed she loved shoes almost as much as music.

I stopped and wondered why I was thinking of her in the past tense. The evidence didn't point that way. But her mother believed it and maybe that pessimism had crept into me.

I wandered over to the vanity. Most girls had pictures of their best friends or boyfriends stuck in the frame of their mirror. Sierra had old men. Old men with musical instruments. They were probably famous, but not to me.

I flipped through the papers on her desk. From the looks of it, her mother didn't spend too much time on math during homeschooling, because Sierra bombed her last test. Though she got a perfect score in science. I looked for notes or anything personal in the pile, but found only schoolwork.

This was certainly not the desk she wrote her good-bye note on, though. The desk in my vision was dark wood. This one was white.

I wandered around the room, my fingers grazing all the surfaces, knobs, and switches. It brought up nothing interesting. Sierra spent a lot of time alone, in silence, or with classical music in the background.

"Want to rub your hands along the bed?" Justin asked, wagging his eyebrows.

I flashed him a look.

He smiled. "Just being helpful."

I dropped to my hands and knees and peered under the bed. An indistinct form was bundled in the darkness. I reached my hand in and pulled it out.

The bed squeaked as Justin got up. "Find something?"

"Just an overnight bag." I lifted it up and onto the bed.

"See if anything's in it."

I unzipped it and the handles fell open. "Empty."

I gripped the handles again, about to bring them back together, when I felt that familiar buzzing feeling of a vision coming to the surface. I focused in on it and heard a voice.

"How many days will you be gone this time?" a girl asked.

The voice was somewhat familiar.

"Only three," Sierra responded, shoving a pair of shoes into the corner of the overnight bag with one hand, while the other gripped the handle.

"It must be terrible," the girl said.

Sierra tossed a pair of jeans into the bag. *"It's not so bad. There's a piano at each house."*

"Well, I'll miss you."

"I'll miss you, too," Sierra answered, zipping up the bag. Then she turned to say good-bye to her friend.

Despite the fact that her hair wasn't dyed black yet and her eyes were makeup free, I immediately recognized the face of Mallory Neely.

Sierra's friend. My friend. The one who'd told me, despite living next door to Sierra her whole life, that she hardly knew her.

NINETEEN

I STOOD AT MY LOCKER, PULLING OUT BOOKS AND watching the stream of kids go by. I was keeping one eye out for Mallory.

She had a lot of explaining to do.

Why hadn't she told me that she and Sierra were friends? Apparently close friends at that. Close enough to chitchat about the perils of having divorced parents while Sierra packed to visit her father.

I felt a tap on my shoulder and turned, ready to tear into Mallory. Instead, Kendra stood eyeing me suspiciously.

"People are talking," she said.

Vague much? "About what?"

"The cockroach in Tiffany's locker, Cody's car . . ." Her voice trailed off.

I shrugged. "Yeah, so?" I didn't get her point.

She arched her finely manicured brows. "They *are* your biggest enemies."

"Not by my choice. I'd love to live my life with no enemies at all." I paused, finally understanding what she was getting at. "Wait, what are you saying?"

"It's not what *I'm* saying. It's other people."

I suppressed a groan. Did I have to pull this out of her? "What are other people saying, then?"

"They're starting to wonder if you're getting back at the popular crowd."

I leaned back against the locker and let out an exaggerated sigh. I was being put on the defensive. Again. Well, at least it was a familiar place. "They think *I* did those things?" I scoffed. "Please. Over the years, Tiffany and Cody have racked up a high number of people who have reason to seek revenge on them."

Kendra narrowed her eyes. "But all those other kids wouldn't be able to pull it off."

"And I would?"

"No one knows Tiffany's locker combination."

"Neither do I," I snapped.

"But couldn't you just put your hand on the locker?" She made woo-woo motions with her fingers. "And get a vision of Tiffany spinning the dial and memorize her combination?"

"It doesn't work that perfectly —"

Kendra interrupted, "But it's possible, right?"

I pressed the palm of my hand against my forehead as the stirrings of a headache formed in my temple. I had to clench my jaw to force myself to keep my tone level. "Why would I do that? Why now when things aren't that bad for me?"

"Tiffany says it's because you think you can get away with it now. She says you think we'll back you up."

My frustration boiled over. "Don't you see what she's doing?" I snapped. "Tiffany has made it quite clear she hates that people are friendly with me now. She wants me to return to outcast status. She wants to turn everyone against me again. She probably put that cockroach in her locker herself."

I slammed the locker door closed and slid my books into the crook of my arm. "I've got to get to class."

Kendra put her hand on my arm. "Wait. I don't believe what Tiffany's saying."

I hesitated. "Really?"

"Someone could have snuck into the office and snagged her locker combo. It could be anyone. I don't think it's you."

"Thanks," I said truthfully.

I was only slightly relieved, though. Kendra might have believed me, but the rest of the school? It would be Tiffany's word against mine. And I had no doubt it was Tiffany who had started the rumor in the first place.

"Listen," Kendra said. "I'm having a party tomorrow night. I want you to come."

I blinked quickly. I'd never been to a house party before. Never even been invited. And my gut was telling me I didn't want to go to this one, either. But I'd made a deal with my mother. And a deal's a deal.

I forced a smile. "Sure, I'll come."

Kendra looked pleased. "Great." As an afterthought, she added, "Obviously, don't bring Mallory."

"What? Why?"

Kendra gave me a look that said it should have been obvious. "That girl is crazysauce."

"What do you mean?"

"Have you seen the way she looks at you? Get a clue, Clare. Lose the psycho."

I didn't see Mallory all day. She was either sick or she skipped. As I walked home, thoughts churned in my head. People at school thought Mallory was nuts. But they'd also branded me as a freak for most of my life, so I didn't put much stock in their opinions. But Mallory *had* lied to me about Sierra.

I needed to know why.

Just then, Mallory's house came into view. I couldn't solve my other problems right now, but I could get some answers on this one.

Mrs. Neely welcomed me with a smile and told me to go right upstairs to Mallory's room. I knocked on the door and heard a soft, "Come in."

Mallory's room looked like a place in transition. Her bed had once held a canopy, but it had been taken down. The walls were white, and a pink flowered border was in the process of being torn down, by obviously unprofessional hands.

"What are you doing here?" Mallory peeked out from under a giant pink comforter.

I stepped closer to her. "Are you sick?"

"No," she croaked.

"Then why didn't you go to school? Why are you lying in bed?"

After a pause, she said, "I saw you."

The words were so soft, I wasn't even sure if they were meant for me. "What?"

"I saw you go into Sierra's house yesterday. Mrs. Waldman had you do your psychic thing, didn't she?"

"Yeah, so?"

Mallory propped herself up on her elbows and looked at me. "So that's why I skipped school today. I didn't want to be there when you told everyone what I did."

My heart felt heavy with foreboding as I sat on the end of Mallory's bed, looking into her panicked eyes. "What did you do?"

Mallory balled her hands into fists and pressed them against her eyes. "It's my fault, okay! It's my fault she left."

"You *were* friends?" I already knew the truth, but wanted to hear it from her.

Mallory sniffled and took a deep breath. "She was my only friend, and for a long time, I was hers. Then she started to change. I was so excited when she said the homeschooling thing was ending and she was going to go to Eastport High. I thought, finally, I'd have a friend at school, too, instead of just at home."

"What happened?"

"She never spoke to me at school. I think she realized how low I was on the social ladder and I was a grade behind her and she was embarrassed to be seen with me."

I crossed my arms. "Well, that's pretty shitty."

"You want to know something pathetic?" Mallory sat up fully and leaned back against the headboard. "I still tried to see her after school. Be her secret friend, you know? I figured that was better than nothing. But she never had time for me anymore. She was always staying after school for projects and stuff."

I frowned. "What does that have to do with her leaving?"

"Eventually, it all built up inside and one day I went to her house and we had a huge blowup." Her voice cracked. "I said every mean thing I'd ever held back. And then she left. Without a word to me and only that little note for her mom."

No wonder Mallory never wanted to talk about Sierra. She was hurting and, on top of that, she blamed herself for everything. I still wished she'd been honest with me from the start, but at least I understood now.

I softened my voice. "I don't think one fight with a friend would make someone do something so drastic as run away. You shouldn't blame yourself."

Mallory stared down at her fuzzy blanket, picking at some lint. "I know you're looking for Sierra." Her eyes lifted to mine. "Will you do me a favor? If you find her, even if she doesn't want to come back, just tell her I'm sorry. That I didn't mean all the things I said. I was just hurt, so I lashed out."

"I will," I said. "I promise."

TWENTY

MOM NEARLY FELL OVER WHEN I TOLD HER I WAS going to a party. You'd think I'd said I was secretly an alien from the planet Vespar. But I understood her reaction. This was a first in Clare Land.

When her voice returned after the initial shock, she went into Mom mode. Her eyes narrowed. "How are you getting there?"

We were in my room, and I was looking through my closet. "Brooke's going to pick me up."

"Are this girl's parents going to be home?"

I considered lying, but if Mom listened to my thoughts and caught me, I'd be grounded. So I went with the honest approach. I turned to face her. "I really don't know."

She folded her arms. "Will there be drinking at this party?"

"I assume so, but, Mom, you know *I* won't." Drinking meant a lack of control and I wasn't putting myself through that. Especially considering my admirer-slash-stalker could be at the party.

After a mini-lecture and a double-pinky-swear promise

that I wouldn't get in a car with someone who'd been drinking, *and* that I would call her if I needed her, Mom agreed to let me go. Then she immediately transformed from nervous to thrilled. She said she was happy to see me getting out there and doing normal teen stuff instead of spending another weekend in with Perry and Nate.

She tore through my closet, picking out five different outfits and forcing me to put on a little fashion show for her. All five elicited responses along the lines of "Boring," "Yawn," and "Don't you own anything that isn't black or brown?" Eventually she approved of a shirred violet top and my skinny jeans.

Mom was enjoying herself so much that I even let her do my makeup. I usually never wore anything but lip gloss, preferring the natural look. But I had to admit the liner, mascara, and shadow Mom ringed my eyes with really made the blue pop. I let my curls hang loose down my shoulders and put a little extra anti-frizz serum in for some shine. Then I stepped back and looked in the full-length mirror.

"Wow," Mom said.

And I kind of agreed.

"Now, remember." I smirked. "This means the next time Phil asks you out, you have to say yes."

"Yeah, yeah," Mom replied, but she didn't seem too put out. In fact, I think I saw a hint of a smile at the edges of her mouth.

I sat around flipping channels while waiting for Brooke, who'd texted me to say she was running "a little late." Finally, she beeped the horn and I was on my way to my first party. A concoction of equal parts excitement and terror swirled in my stomach.

Kendra's giant McMansion was set at the end of the dead-end road, up on a hill. It seemed to glower down at the rest of the more modest McMansions with its judgy little window-eyes. The driveway looked like a freeway in one of those apocalyptic movies where everyone's gone, but their cars are left behind, haphazardly parked this way and that. One even had the door left open.

I wondered why it looked like we were the last to arrive, when Brooke was supposedly Kendra's best friend. But as I watched her primp in the rearview mirror, I figured it out. Brooke wanted to make an entrance.

"When Jordan sees me, he's going to be so sorry about our fight, he'll get down on his knees and beg for me back." She turned to me with a devious smile and I smiled back, hoping that was the right response.

As we walked up to the front door, the music boomed louder and louder, as did my scared little heart.

Brooke let out a delighted sigh. "I love it when Kendra's dad has business trips." Then she opened the door and walked in, a few steps in front of me, flipping her hair and swishing her hips.

All eyes were on her as she sauntered down the hallway. Before I knew it, she had disappeared into a swarm of male admirers, and I was left alone to navigate the maze that was Kendra's house. I closed the door behind me, suddenly having second thoughts. I may have been invited, but that didn't mean I belonged.

Last Year Clare would have a lot to say to This Year Clare if she could have peeked into the future and seen me in Kendra Kiger's house. She'd probably slap me upside the head and say some variation of "Hey, Future Clare, wtf?"

I reminded myself of my deal with Mom and started walking. Music blared from the front living room, where a group of sweaty bodies writhed to the beat. Two girls danced on a glass coffee table with their eyes closed. My first thought was how unsafe that was, which pretty much explains why I'd never been to a party before. The kitchen was next, and from the line that trailed out of it, I guessed that's where the keg was. I peeked in, looking for any friendly face, then ducked back out.

The hallway continued to the right, but noise emanated from a doorway that led downstairs to the basement. I took the stairs slowly and my eyes widened when I reached the bottom. This was where the party really was.

The basement was large and finished, spotted with couches and beanbag chairs, and a pool table. Clusters of kids everywhere. I heard someone call my name and saw Kendra waving to me from the corner. Tiffany stood next to her with a sneer on her face.

I took a deep breath and threaded my way through the crowd, practicing opening lines in my head. *Great party? I like your house?* Ugh. But I didn't get a chance to pick one because Tiffany spoke first, of course waiting until I was in hearing range.

"You invited *her*?" Tiffany scoffed.

Kendra rolled her eyes. "Get over it, Tiff."

Tiffany looked back at me, sharply. "Where's your shadow?"

"Who?" I asked flatly.

"Your little girlfriend? Mallory Neely?"

"Oh, shut it, Tiffany," I hissed back furiously.

"Mallory's got a big fat crush on you," she continued, her eyes alight with fiery loathing. "She wants to take you to the homecoming dance."

I was hoping Kendra would back me up and tell Tiffany to let it go, but instead she said, "Tiffany's right, Clare. That Mallory girl is loony."

"She follows you around like a puppy dog," Tiffany added, as if she really cared about my social well-being.

"I think it's time that puppy got kicked." Kendra snickered and Tiffany joined in with a cackle.

I felt sick. I opened my mouth, ready to unload on them, but Justin picked that moment to call to me from across the room. Lucky for Kendra and Tiffany, I walked away.

"Hey!" he said, pulling me into a huge, unexpected hug, as if he hadn't seen me in months.

I extricated myself after a moment and responded with a lackluster, "Hey, yourself."

Justin beamed at me. "Wow, I saw you and Tiffany chatting. No hair pulling or anything!"

"Just because it didn't happen, doesn't mean I didn't want to," I muttered.

He laughed, a little too loud. My joke wasn't *that* funny.

But then I realized he was swaying in place where he stood. The drink in his hand obviously wasn't his first of the evening.

I looked over his shoulder and spied Gabriel standing with two other guys I recognized from the hockey team. His eyes found mine and he lifted his plastic cup in greeting. I smiled and nodded once in return.

Justin glanced behind him to see who I was smiling at, then turned back to me, frowning. He edged closer and asked me a question. I couldn't hear him over the music, so I pointed to my ear. He leaned in closer and yelled, "You want a drink?"

I shook my head back and forth. "Nah, I'm all set. Thanks."

"So was Mallory Neely your stalker the whole time?"

I stepped back. "Where did you hear that?"

His face changed, perhaps realizing he'd let something slip that he shouldn't have. "Oh, Tiffany mentioned that she saw Mallory put that picture in your locker."

I skipped the whole part about how I knew Mallory wasn't the stalker and got right to the Tiffany part. "So she's 'the little birdie' you've been getting all your info from?"

He put his hand up. "I'm not friends with her or anything. She just walked up to me and told me."

I believed him, but still, it brought up things I'd worked hard to forget.

"Don't let her get to you," Justin said.

"Easier said than done."

"Just think of it this way. Anytime Tiffany Desposito gets a rise out of you, evil wins."

My mouth twitched.

His finger trailed along my lip. "Is that a smile I see?"

I playfully batted his hand away. "No."

"Yes, I think it was."

I could see Gabriel watching us, his face dark and unreadable. Justin's arm snaked around my waist, pulling me in to him.

"Isn't this great?" Justin asked.

"The party?" I didn't really know. I had no other parties to compare it to.

"Not just the party. Everything. Me here with my friends, you here with your friends." He leaned closer and whispered in my ear, "This is what it could be like, you know. If we got back together. It would be different this time."

Different this time? I pulled away. "Funny, I liked how it was *last* time," I said indignantly. "Before *you* went ahead and cheated on me with that trashy —"

Justin cut me off. "Don't take it the wrong way. Come on."

A kid passed by. "Clare, it's your hero!" he called out.

Justin's face lit up and he accepted the praise in a dramatic bow. I cringed. I really hoped we weren't going to have to tell the story again. Obviously, I was grateful for what Justin did that day last summer. And I was more than grateful that he'd lived to tell the tale. But I didn't want to talk about it with people circling around, hanging on every word. That's what it was like when school started, and I'd hoped everyone would be over it by now.

But Justin liked it.

Right there in Kendra's basement, he told the story again, loudly and with flourish, as I stared at the floor. I hated being the center of attention.

Justin fed the crowd with the right words at the right time. He was so happy and at home in this world.

But not me.

No matter how many of these parties I ended up going to, it would never feel comfortable to me.

I glanced back at where Gabriel had stood with a couple guys, but instead two girls now surrounded him.

Brooke and Tiffany.

Brooke was just giving him the same dreamy, appreciative gaze she always did. Tiffany took it one step further, stepping closer to finger the collar of his shirt as she spoke, her head tilted to the side, a sly smile spreading across her lips.

Gabriel's face stayed blank and uninterested, but my chest suddenly felt heavy. As Tiffany ran her fingers down his sleeve, my insides squeezed.

"Hellooooo . . . Clare?"

From the expectant look on Justin's face, I realized he'd asked me a question. But I couldn't talk. A lump had lodged in my throat. Instead, I excused myself and went up to the main floor to find the bathroom.

The line was a mile long. I really didn't need to go. I just wanted to get away and be alone for a minute.

"What's taking so long?" a girl whined.

"Someone's barfing in there," a guy said as he headed out through the sliding glass doors to the backyard. He didn't have to wait in line. As a guy, the world was his urinal.

"I wonder if there's another bathroom upstairs." The whiny girl was jumping in place now.

"We're not allowed up there," another girl shot back.

Someplace empty where I could process my jealousy and other conflicted feelings in peace? Sounded like the perfect place for me.

My hand trailed up the white banister as I climbed the stairs. Of course, there wasn't a speck of dust on my fingers when I lifted them. Everything about Kendra's house was perfect, just like her life. One of the richest girls in town. One of the most popular girls in school. She didn't have to work all summer long in a candlelit room. Her only problem was deciding which of her thousand outfits to wear each day.

I reached the landing and turned down a long, expansive hallway with many closed doors. I didn't want to go opening random bedroom doors. I figured the bathroom had to have been left open, though, so I crept down the hall.

I found it and laid my hand on the doorjamb. It was empty and quiet. For the first time that night, I felt like I could relax. I closed my eyes and let out a deep breath.

And a vision wavered to the surface.

Kendra standing in her jeans and bra. She pleaded, "Come on, Mom. People are going to get here soon. Let me go downstairs."

"Not until you are finished," a voice snapped back. "Try that one. It'll look better than the other."

The vision must have been from the point of view of Kendra's mother gripping the doorjamb while her daughter changed in front of her.

Kendra picked up a shirt from the floor. Had it been thrown there? *She pulled it over her head.*

Her mother's thoughts were vile.

Looking good doesn't just happen.

I saw her eat that cheeseburger the other day.

No wonder those jeans are too tight.

Her mother looked down to compare her own body to her daughter's. She was skinny, but not in a good way. More in a desperate, pitiful way. I wanted to feed her a bag of chips. A tight shirt clung to her obviously lifted boobs, and trendy designer jeans hung on her emaciated hips. She was clinging to her youth, perhaps trying to live vicariously through her daughter.

I've never seen Brooke eat a cheeseburger.

I've tried to teach this girl. Doesn't she want to be on the Homecoming Court like I was?

I sized up Kendra's mother pretty quickly. She was one of those super-competitive women with nothing to show for her own accomplishments so she pushed her children harder and harder in order to claim their accomplishments as her own. If Kendra won a crown on homecoming, Kendra's mother would have bragging rights with all the other rich, youth-obsessed moms in her clique.

As the vision faded to black, I suddenly felt a longing to be with my own mother, laughing on the couch while watching TV, sharing a tub of ice cream with two spoons.

Kendra might have had a lot of material things that I didn't, but I wouldn't trade places with her. Not for one second.

By the time I came back downstairs, the party had gotten even rowdier. People were dancing on the pool table, making out on the couch. And, from the smell of it, someone had puked in the large potted plant in the corner.

Kendra was dancing and laughing. Little did most people know, her life was far from perfect. I had no desire to tell her about my vision and have a friendly heart-to-heart about it. I still trusted that girl as far as I could throw her.

But the vision, at least, explained a lot.

I stood alone, wringing my hands because I didn't know what else to do with them. Gabriel came up behind me with one eyebrow raised. "Enjoying yourself?"

"Yeah," I said sarcastically. "This is *so* my scene."

I looked around at everyone having an effortlessly good time. I wasn't anything like those girls. Most of the time it didn't bother me, but at that moment, I wondered. What would it be like to blend in? To be blond or brunette, with stick-straight hair and not my unruly red curls. To not be psychic. To be normal. To fit in.

Gabriel studied me for a moment. "You don't realize it, do you?"

I blinked, twice. "Realize what?"

"What makes you different makes you beautiful."

My breath caught in my throat.

I met his gaze and his eyes were sincere. Gorgeous. Smoldering. My heart fluttered wildly in my chest.

Gabriel's lips parted as if to speak.

Then the lights blinked on and off. Everyone froze and turned to look at Kendra, who stood on the pool table.

Kendra yelled, "Can I have everyone's attention, please?"

The room went silent.

Kendra's eyes panned the area, found mine, and then a slow smile spread on her face. "I've thrown a lot of parties before, but I have a special present for you tonight."

A couple guys whooped.

"Our friend Clare Fern is here." Kendra pointed to me, and I immediately knew this wasn't good. "You all know that Clare is psychic. And I bet that if we cheer her on, she could do some readings for us tonight. What do you guys think?"

The room exploded into drunken cheers and clumsy clapping. All eyes went to me as I stood dumbfounded. People stepped back, forming a circle around me. Only Gabriel was left by my side.

"No . . . no . . . thanks," I said.

"Oh, come on!" Kendra cheered, but her eyes glittered with disdain.

Why was she doing this? She knew I didn't want to do readings for her. I'd told her enough times.

All their stares bored into me. I was on display. The circus freak in the center ring. My instinct had been right all along. They wanted no part of *me*. Only what I could *do*.

"Come on, Clare!"

"Me first!"

Voices chattered around me, and the room began to tilt and spin. I turned to look for Gabriel, but even he wasn't beside me anymore. I was alone. I scanned the faces. Brooke was wrapped around Jordan in the corner, oblivious. Tiffany stood behind Cody, whispering into his ear as he smiled wickedly, their narrowed eyes glued to me.

I searched and searched until, finally, I found Justin in the crowd. He glowed proudly.

"Come on, Clare, show 'em what you can do," he said encouragingly.

Why didn't he understand I wanted no part of this? I didn't want to be the entertainment. I wanted to be a regular kid in the crowd.

Just when I thought I couldn't take another second, the lights went out. Girls screamed overdramatically. Guys cheered as if it were a fun game.

And somewhere in the darkness, a hand reached out and clasped mine.

A voice whispered in my ear, "Let's go."

TWENTY-ONE

I ALLOWED THE STRONG, WARM HAND TO LEAD ME
out of the dark chaos inside Kendra's house and into the surprisingly bright night outside. The moon was almost full and
its light illuminated Gabriel's face.

He hadn't abandoned me. He'd left my side to shut off the
lights, creating a distraction so I could disappear.

"Want to go? My Jeep's right over there." He motioned
over his shoulder.

I glanced at the red plastic cup in his hand.

"It's water," he said, noticing my hesitation. He dumped
the remainder on the grass and tossed the cup toward a trash
bin. "I have a game tomorrow."

"Oh," I said, relieved. "Yeah, let's get out of here."

We drove in silence for a little while. I didn't want to talk
about what had happened. The embarrassment was too fresh.
Gabriel seemed to sense that, so he turned on the radio and
stayed quiet.

Passing streetlights lit up his face for brief moments, and I
took peeks at him when I could. The lines of his jaw. His

intensely dark eyes. He caught me looking, and I glanced away quickly.

"Want me to drop you off at your house?" he asked. "Or," he added with hope in his voice, "would you like to go somewhere?"

I glanced at the clock in the dashboard. I still had an hour before curfew. And I didn't want to go home. All night I'd felt out of place and uncomfortable. It was only just now, with Gabriel, that I'd started to feel like myself again.

"Let's go to the beach," I suggested.

Minutes later, Gabriel parallel parked in a metered spot and we gazed out at the boardwalk and the beach beyond it. Town Beach was flat with white sand and a sprinkling of sea-shells. Perfect for the tourists (and the town, which charged fifteen dollars a day to park in summer). There were more cars than I expected. But it was a mild fall night and the beauty of the full moon's reflection on the water seemed to pull people like the moon itself pulled the tides.

I frowned. I didn't want to be with random people milling about and smacking their lips against each other while I tried to listen to Gabriel's words.

I wanted to be alone with him.

"Start the car," I said, making a decision. His face fell in disappointment until I added, "I've got a better place to go."

Just a bit farther past the shops, down a couple tree-lined residential roads, and at the end of a dead-end street was another beach. The sand was too rocky to go barefoot. The water was thick with seaweed. But a line of pines hid the beach from view, and tall sand dunes topped with prickly beach grass made the descent intimidating. So when you got down, it was worth it, because you could be alone. Even if another townie was there, sunbathing or fishing off the jetty, there was enough room that you still felt like you had your own slice of paradise. Removed from the flurry and noise of the real world. You could stare out at the vastness of the sea, the infinite line of the horizon, and feel so small. Feel that, in the scheme of things, maybe your giant problems weren't so significant.

Hidden Beach, as townies called it, was too far for me to walk, so I'd only been there with Perry or Mom now and then when the summer crowds had gotten to us. I'd never been there in the fall and never at night.

I told Gabriel where to park but didn't tell him any more, taking delight in his utter confusion.

"Where are we going?" Gabriel called after me as I gleefully jumped down from his Jeep and ran toward the tree line.

"You'll see," I teased over my shoulder.

He caught up to me just as we broke through the wall of trees. Then he gasped at the sight before us.

"What is this place?"

"Hidden Beach," I said, staring at the dark expanse of the sea below us.

"I didn't even know this was here."

"You're an official townie now," I said. "You're in on the secret."

I expected him to crack a joke, but instead a flash of sadness settled onto his face, then quickly left.

"Here," he said, holding out his hand. "I'll help you down."

We navigated the sand dunes, following a well-worn trail. He descended the steep slope with me close behind. I slipped near the bottom, crashing into him. He steadied us both while I laughed nervously.

We reached the rocky shore, but before we could take it all in, we were plunged into darkness. A cloud had covered the moon. At Town Beach, the lights from stores and streetlamps would have still shimmered in the distance, but Hidden Beach was deserted and sunken. No light reached it now.

The black was all-encompassing. I couldn't see the shoreline. The only way I knew the ocean was to my left was from the sounds of the waves pounding the sand.

Suddenly, even though I was cloaked in darkness, I had the eerie feeling of being watched. I had the sudden thought that anything, any sort of monster or nightmare, could crawl out of the sea and be edging toward me and I'd never know. It was an irrational fear.

"Where are you?" Gabriel whispered.

I reached my hands out, utterly blind, until my palms hit his chest. Then the cloud cover moved, and the moon shone on us like a spotlight. I pulled my hands back and wrapped my arms around myself.

It was cooler down here and my thin shirt did little to protect me from the ocean winds. I shivered and rubbed my upper arms.

Before I even knew what he was doing, Gabriel had stripped off his hooded sweatshirt, leaving himself in only a black T-shirt. He held it out to me. "Wear this."

Perry would disown me for wearing a Yankees sweatshirt, but he would never know, and I was too cold to care about team loyalty. I pulled it over my head and inhaled deeply when I recognized Gabriel's scent.

Now I'd never want to give it back.

"That's better," I said. "Thanks."

Tangled strands of red hair whipped around my face with each gust of wind. Gabriel tried to trap them behind my ears, but they just broke free and flew away again. I giggled. He pulled me closer and put his arms around me from behind. We stood staring at the black metallic waves rushing forward and retreating again in a kind of rhythmic dance.

I wondered what Gabriel was thinking about.

I didn't have to wonder for too long.

"He doesn't understand you like I do," he said, his breath warm against my neck.

Tonight, anyway, Gabriel was right about that. When Kendra had put me on the spot and humiliated me, Justin had cheered me on.

Gabriel was the one who'd saved me.

But then I remembered that day last summer again. The gun. Justin stepping in front of me.

I turned around to face Gabriel.

As if he could sense where my mind had gone, he said, "It's because of what happened, isn't it? That's why you can't give up on him. Why you won't move on. Because he was there that day and he tried to save you."

"It isn't a small thing, Gabriel," I explained.

"I'm not asking you to overlook it. Hell, even I'm grateful to the guy for what he did. I'm just asking you to be sure you know what you're doing. Check your motivation. There's a difference between love and obligation."

I stared down at the smooth rocks on the sand. "I know I'm not obligated to him."

Do I know that, though? If Justin hadn't nearly died for me, would I really be considering giving him a second chance? Would I really be considering choosing him over Gabriel?

Gabriel reached out and brushed my cheek. "I shouldn't have said anything."

I shrugged. I didn't want to talk about Justin with him. I didn't want to think about Justin when I was with him. I wished I could keep the two separate.

Gabriel took a deep breath. "You know, all this bravado, it's an act. I want to be with you, but I don't know who you belong with. And if you decide Justin's your guy, then that's fine with me."

"And we'd still be friends?" I asked skeptically.

"Sure," he said, though something in his eyes said no. Like he already had a plan in place for what he'd do if I chose Justin.

I appreciated that Gabriel never pressured me. Never gave me an ultimatum. I knew he had other interested girls waiting on the sidelines. Tiffany had basically thrown herself at him at the party. He didn't have to wait around for me to make up my mind.

But, so far, he had.

I threw my arms around his neck and squeezed him in a big friendly hug. He laughed, taken aback by my sudden attack of affection.

But I didn't let go, and the hug morphed from something friendly into something else. My hands trailed down his back, tracing his muscles through his T-shirt. I breathed against the heat of his neck, my lips almost touching his skin.

"You'd better stop doing that," he said. His voice was different, raspy.

I leaned back and looked up into his eyes, but I didn't let go of him.

It was almost a dare.

His fingers locked into my hair, gently pulling my head back to tilt my mouth up. I closed my eyes as our lips touched.

He kissed me warily at first, and then — when I didn't pull away — hungrily, like a kiss he'd been storing up for weeks. Warmth radiated out from my lips, down my neck, and through my entire body like a spreading fire.

My mind was unsure, but my body wasn't. I didn't want our kissing to end. Ever. It felt too good.

Gabriel broke the kiss first. I took a gasp of fresh air. My lips felt tingly and swollen. He looked into my eyes intently, his gaze serious.

This was it. This was the moment. He was going to put

me on the spot. Ask me to choose. My heart sped up. I didn't know what to do, how to answer.

"My mother's still here."

I stepped back, not expecting that statement in the least. "That's nice," I stammered, wondering why he felt the need to say that at a moment like this.

"She came here for a reason."

"Oh?" *A reason more than just to see him?*

He looked away from me, at the ocean. "She's sober now."

"Gabriel, that's fantastic," I said enthusiastically. Though as the words left my mouth, I realized Gabriel wasn't exactly jumping for joy. There was more to this.

He turned back to me, and I saw it in his face. I sensed the words coming before he even opened his mouth. My stomach clenched.

"She wants me to move back home with her." He swallowed hard. "To New York."

I took a sharp intake of air. A thick cloud passed over the moon again, slowly, and the dunes behind Gabriel seemed to slide and erode before my eyes, until they disappeared in the black.

"What are you going to do?" I asked.

From the surrounding darkness, Gabriel said, "Honestly? I don't know."

TWENTY-TWO

IT WAS SUNDAY, LATE MORNING, AND MOM WAS flitting around the kitchen, making a racket. I'd offered to help make brunch, but she'd shooed me away, so I took a big mug of hot chocolate out to the porch swing. The front yard was so covered with Halloween decorations, it was almost comical. One of them had fallen over. Looked like the ceramic Frankenstein, maybe. I made a mental note to fix it later. For now, I wrapped a blanket around my shoulders and watched the clouds move across the sky.

Last night was both wonderful and awful, in almost equal amounts. Kendra had humiliated me. Justin had disappointed me. Gabriel had wowed me. And then I was hit with the worst news of all.

Gabriel might be leaving.

And I didn't want to lose him now. I'd always felt that even if I chose Justin, I might still get to keep Gabriel in my life. As a friend. But now everything had changed. Keeping or losing Gabriel wasn't in my control anymore. And I hated that.

I took a sip of my cocoa. It was too hot and burned my

throat on its way down. I set it on the railing to cool for a bit and thought more about the party.

What was up with Justin? It was like he was two people, one when we were alone and another when he was with the popular crowd. Had he always been that way and I hadn't known? During our relationship, we'd never hung out with his friends. I never got to see how he acted with them.

Last night was what he'd always wanted: to have me *and* the parties. But a party was where we'd ended. A party was where he got drunk and hooked up with Tiffany.

As if I'd conjured him with my thoughts, Justin appeared at the end of my driveway. I blinked a few times, wondering if I'd fallen asleep and was dreaming this, but as he climbed the porch steps, the wood creaking beneath his shoes, I knew it was real.

His confident swagger was gone, replaced by a timid wariness, like a child stepping out of time-out. He sat beside me, and the porch swing rocked back and forth with the shifting weight.

"I'm so sorry," he said, his voice low.

"For what?" I wanted to know if he understood how much he'd let me down.

"I just . . . I think . . ." He stumbled over his words as he started. "I didn't realize how you felt, until you were gone. I thought about it the rest of the night and I wanted to kick myself. It's all I could think about this morning. I was going to call but decided to just come over. I had to apologize in person."

"The party scene," I began, "it's just not me."

"I know that. I would never force you to go. But I was so excited that you were there and I didn't realize you hated it. And I shouldn't have cheered you on when Kendra put you on the spot. I just . . . got caught up in how happy I was to have you there and didn't realize how you were feeling until it was too late."

I wrapped the blanket tighter around myself. Justin would never hurt me on purpose. What did I expect? He wasn't a mind reader like my mother. Maybe I'd been too hard on him.

When I didn't speak, he continued, "What happened this summer . . . nearly dying . . . it made me want to enjoy every minute of every day. That's why I've been trying so hard to win you back."

"I know," I said, softening.

"Maybe last night, I was trying to enjoy myself too much." He laughed lightly at himself, and I gave him a little smile.

Was it so horrible that Justin was a fun-loving guy? He loved to laugh and hang with his friends. Was that so bad? He made me laugh, too.

I met his eyes directly. "It's okay."

He didn't look convinced, though. He looked forlorn.

He cupped my face with both hands, gently, as if it were something invaluable. As if *I* were invaluable.

Then, before I could stop him, he leaned in and kissed me.

I'd kissed Justin a million times last year and once this summer, but I still wasn't expecting it to happen again now. The kiss was familiar and sweet. It unearthed memories like a storm dredges up treasures from the ocean. Some ugly, like seaweed. Some beautiful, like smoothed stones and seashells.

He released me and looked deep into my eyes, as if he were searching for something. An answer to a question he'd silently asked. I stared, openmouthed, unsure of how to act or what to say.

He smiled sadly. "I just wanted to do that one more time. In case you pick him."

Then he descended the porch stairs and went on his way.

I was left alone with my fingertips on my lips, wondering if that was the last kiss Justin and I would ever share.

Monday was the first day of Spirit Week and everyone dressed in a hippie theme. Mostly, people wore tie-dyed shirts and the peace symbol. It would have been easy for me to find something from the horror that was my mom's closet, but I'd forgotten. And, once again, I didn't fit in.

Mallory was feeling better. After spilling the truth to me about her fight with Sierra, her guilt had lessened. I took the credit for her return to normalcy. Normal for her, anyway.

"Where's your school spirit, Clare?" she said, leaning up against a locker. She wore black almost every day.

I arched an eyebrow at her hypocrisy.

Mallory threw her head back and laughed. "I'm just kidding. Spirit Week is lame. I'm with you. We're rebels." She held her fist out for me to bump it.

"Actually," I said, struggling to pull a book from the

bottom of the pile without toppling the whole tower, "I was going to go with the theme today. I just forgot."

"Oh." Mallory's kohl-rimmed eyes stared at the floor.

"Oh, whatever," I said, scoffing. "If you were really so antiestablishment, you wouldn't be all pumped up to go to the dance."

"I'm *not* going to the dance," she countered.

"Why not?"

"You're not going."

"So? Didn't you have someone you wanted to ask?"

She shook her head quickly. "It's too much of a long shot. I don't want to ask anymore. It would just cause problems."

I was about to request details, but Brooke came up to me with that look she got when she had gossip she compulsively needed to share. She gave Mallory the death stare until Mallory muttered, "Catch you later, Clare," and stormed off.

"Did you hear what happened?" Brooke said.

I didn't want to be completely rude to her. It was Kendra who'd pissed me off. But I didn't want any part of her gossip grapevine, either. I faced my locker. "I've got to get to class, Brooke."

She stepped in my line of vision. "Kendra is broken-hearted!"

Huh? Because I'm mad at her? "You think I care? After what she did to me at the party?"

Brooke shook her head. "She tried to get you some attention, that's all. And you froze up and blew it. No biggie. Everyone forgot five minutes later."

I rolled my eyes. "Then what's she upset about?"

"Tiffany asked Brendan to the dance."

I could barely keep up with these girls' love lives. "I thought Kendra was going to ask him."

"She was. And Tiffany knew that. But she did it anyway."

"Wow, you mean Tiffany's an evil wench? I'm shocked. Shocked, I tell you!" I patted my heart in faux surprise.

Brooke rolled her eyes. "I know Tiffany's always been mean to you, but Kendra was her best friend. Who does that to a best friend?"

"I don't know," I said, cradling my books in my arms as I closed my locker with my elbow. "You three are the worst best friends I've ever seen." After keeping my thoughts to myself for so long, truth suddenly flowed from me like a busted dam. "You're always stabbing each other in the back," I went on. "Tiffany's a man stealer. Kendra insults all of you. And you pretend to be stupid, which is completely disingenuous."

Brooke's mouth opened.

"Big word," I said, "but I know you know what it means."

With that, I spun around and marched down the hall. I headed toward the library, where Mallory and I had study hall. I couldn't wait to tell her what I'd said to Brooke. Mallory would love it.

I entered the library and weaved around the tables until I found her. Mallory sat at a table partially hidden by a shelf that contained all the yearbooks in Eastport High history. She was hunched over a book, gnawing on the end of a pink highlighter. I slid into the empty chair beside her and plopped my books on the table.

"You'll never believe what I just did," I said breathlessly.

Mallory didn't look up. "Let me guess . . . You were at your locker talking to a good friend of yours and an evil bimbo came up and shooed your friend away like she was an annoying little gnat and you did nothing to stop it? Didn't even think to stand up for your friend. Because the other girl was more popular." She looked up with disdain in her eyes. "Did I guess right?"

"No, um," I bumbled. I'd thought Mallory had left because she couldn't stand Brooke. I didn't realize she'd wanted me to say something.

Those girls weren't real friends of mine. Mallory knew that, right?

"I'm sorry, Mallory. But if you just listen, I'll —"

"You're just like Sierra," she spat.

"Excuse me?"

"You acted all sympathetic when I told you how Sierra treated me, but now you're doing the same thing she did. You're friends with me when it's just the two of us, but when your popular friends are around, you treat me like a leper."

My mouth fell open. I was the complete opposite of that and I couldn't believe what Mallory was saying. "That's not true," I said, my voice pleading.

"It *is* true." She stood up, piling her books into her arms. "You're no better than Sierra."

TWENTY-THREE

I LEFT SCHOOL IN A ROTTEN MOOD. I TOOK THE back exit, throwing my body at the metal bar and letting the door slam shut behind me. I trudged down the hill toward the woods in my attempt to avoid all human interaction.

Some trees stood thick, green, and full. Others had begun to change, turning various shades of red, orange, and brown and releasing their leaves, which crunched under my sneakers as I walked the path. The breeze was brisk and cool on my face, reddening my cheeks. Though I was alone and the woods should have seemed quieter than they did when I walked with Mallory, they instead seemed noisier, full of chattering birds and the fluttering of falling leaves. I tried not to bristle at every little sound, reminding myself that nature made noise.

But as I neared the center of the woods, one particular rustle of leaves sounded exactly like a rushing footstep.

I spun to the right. A shadow flashed between the trees.

My heart began to pound hard. "Who's there?" I shouted.

There was no reply. I stared at the spot where I thought I'd seen the shadow, but anything might have caused it — a shaft of light, a passing cloud, the wind moving the branches.

A twig snapped in the opposite direction. I turned slowly in a circle, scanning the trees.

"Mallory? Is that you?" I worked to keep my voice confident. "You don't have to hide from me. We can talk about this."

The woods seemed to hush, as if all the leaves, animals, and underbrush silenced collectively. The thought occurred to me that someone might be out there after all. But not Mallory. My skin broke out in goose bumps.

I turned forward and marched with intensity, eyes panning left and right and occasionally over my shoulder. I stumbled over a knobby root, but quickly regained my balance. I only unclenched my jaw when I reached Fennel Street.

I jogged up to Mallory's door and pounded. No one answered. I looked next door at the Waldmans' house, but the driveway was empty. My only choice was to keep walking home.

No one had emerged from the woods behind me, so they were either done following me or hadn't been there to begin with. I thought about the time I'd heard noises in the house and nearly knifed Perry. There was a good chance this was a similarly silly, paranoid delusion.

By the time my house came into view, my breathing had returned to normal and the fear had left me.

But even if it hadn't, the sight waiting for me in the

driveway was enough to push away any thoughts of a watcher in the woods.

Gabriel leaned up against his Jeep, legs crossed at the ankles, his face lifted to the sky, letting the sun warm his skin.

"Waiting for someone?" I asked.

He opened his eyes and smiled as I came closer. "I wanted to give you a ride home, but I couldn't find you."

"I went out the back and cut through the woods."

"You walked?"

"Yeah, I needed to think."

He straightened. "About what I said?"

"That, and other things." I motioned for him to follow me inside the house.

I swung open the front door, slid my backpack off my shoulder, and dropped it on the floor. Muffled voices emanated from the reading room behind the closed door. I was glad to hear we had a client during the quiet months.

"Mom and Perry must be working," I whispered. "Let's head to the kitchen."

Gabriel followed me. I leaned into the fridge and grabbed two sodas, handing one to him. "So have you made a decision about New York yet?" I asked, trying to sound nonchalant.

"No." He cracked open the soda and took a long sip. "It's hard. I like it here, but my dad is so busy with his job. He'll be fine without me. My mother needs me more."

"But what do *you* want?"

"That's what I have to figure out, I guess."

I knew the feeling.

The phone rang and I sighed, pushing myself off the counter I was leaning against. I took a quick glance at the caller ID. A blocked number. Probably a telemarketer.

"Hello?" I asked.

"Why are you wasting your time with those guys?" The voice was distant and distorted. I couldn't tell if it was male or female.

"Um, I think you have the wrong number."

"No, I don't, Clare." The voice drew my name out. "You belong with me."

Fear uncoiled in my stomach. "Who is this?"

"Good things come to those who wait."

The phone became slippery in my suddenly sweaty hand. "I want you to stop this. Leave me alone."

"I can't do that, Clare. You're so special, unique, and talented. We're meant to be together." The voice added with bold authority, "And we will be."

I slammed the phone down with my trembling hand.

Gabriel rushed to my side. "What was that about?"

At first I didn't answer, my eyes still fixed on the phone. The menacing words echoed in my head as my stomach lurched. Gabriel asked again.

"It was the secret admirer," I said, my voice quivering. "He's gotten more . . . aggressive."

"Wait, what do you mean? I thought it was Justin who gave you that note and the flowers."

"No, it wasn't. And there's been more since then. Someone took a picture of me and left it for me to find. This person's been watching me, maybe following me."

Gabriel's eyes burned with rage. "Why didn't you tell me? No one has the right to scare you like this."

"I'm not scared," I lied. I didn't like feeling vulnerable and didn't like people knowing when I was.

Gabriel put his hands on my shoulders with concern, but his expression changed as he felt my body tremble beneath his fingers. Now he knew how scared I was. I couldn't hide it.

He brought his hands to his sides and his fists clenched, like he wanted to hit something. "When I get my hands on whoever this is —"

"How would you even find out?" I asked hopelessly. "I haven't been able to find out. He's very smart. I've tried to get a vision from the note he put in my locker, the card that came with the flowers, the photo he left for me . . . but I got nothing. He must be wearing gloves every time."

"But you know it's a guy," he said.

"No, I don't. The voice was distorted. It could be anyone."

Gabriel whipped out his cell. "I'm calling my father. It's time to get the police involved."

He went outside to make the call and I sat in the kitchen, twisting my fingers. The caller had seemed less admiring and more . . . angry. Almost as if I had betrayed our imaginary relationship with "those guys" he'd referred to. The night on the beach with Gabriel, I'd felt like someone was watching me. I'd dismissed it as my irrational fear of the dark, but what if my stalker had been out there? Or yesterday, when Justin kissed me on my front porch, in full of view anyone hidden in the trees or in a car parked on the main road. He could have been watching then. He could have been skulking around the woods after school, following me home.

He, or she, could be watching me anywhere at any time.

I pushed the soda away, suddenly nauseous. I felt violated. What kind of person thought that I would be interested in returning his feelings after doing all this creepy stuff?

An insane person, that's who.

The front door clicked softly closed, and a moment later, Gabriel returned to the kitchen, cell phone in his hand, a jumble of emotions on his face.

"What is it?" I asked, rising from my seat.

"My father can't help us with this right now. They have a priority case."

I chuckled nervously. "What, did someone rob the Lobster Cabana again?"

Gabriel shook his head slightly and I knew this was bad news. He wasn't angry at his father's refusal. He was understanding, sad even.

"They found Sierra Waldman's body."

TWENTY-FOUR

NOTHING PUTS YOUR PROBLEMS IN PERSPECTIVE like death. I'd been pitying myself, thinking my stalker issue was the worst problem I could have. Apparently not.

Sierra Waldman was dead. They found her body in the town dump. Though the cause of death hadn't been released yet, people who kill themselves or die accidentally don't end up in the trash. Someone had killed her and dumped her.

I had a bit of a stalker problem, slightly creepy, but most likely harmless. That was nothing compared to what Sierra had been through. What her mother was probably going through right now. I wished I'd been able to help. But, who knows, she may have been dead this whole time.

And the thought that circled through my mind again and again was: *That doesn't mean I still can't help. I can find out who did it.*

But Mom wouldn't want me getting involved. Even I wasn't quite sure I had the guts to go through another murder investigation. But I knew I had the motivation.

I walked through school in a fog all morning, unable to focus on my classes. I searched for Mallory, but it looked like

177

she'd stayed home. I sent her a couple texts, but she didn't reply. I worried about her, but there wasn't anything else I could do until school was over.

People asked me all day long if I was going to work with the cops again. I gave the same reply to everyone. "I don't know. No one asked yet." They didn't seem too torn up over their classmate's death. *Exhilarated* was a better word. Granted no one here really knew her, but they didn't have to revel in the drama of her death like it was a juicy celebrity scandal.

I settled into my seat for physics. It was one of my favorite classes, but I couldn't pay attention. My mind had too much other stuff to process. Sierra's death, my stalker, Gabriel leaving — it all churned in my stomach like spoiled food.

Rylander was going on about impulse, momentum, and something put in motion that could not be stopped. I felt like he was talking about my own life. His eyes landed on me at one point and I felt guilty. Like he knew I wasn't paying a lick of attention to a word he was saying.

I looked down at my notebook.

When class ended, I stood to leave, but Rylander said, "Clare, stay for a moment, will you?"

My heart filled with dread as I returned to my seat and watched the rest of the class file out. Was I in trouble? It wasn't my grades, because I was doing great in this class. Was he going to lay into me for not paying attention? I nervously twirled my pen around in my fingers.

When everyone else was gone, Rylander went over to the

desk beside mine and lifted himself onto it. Kind of a casual way to sit to give someone bad news.

He tapped his chin thoughtfully. "Clare, have you given any thought to a career in science?"

That was about the last thing I expected him to say. "Uh, no."

"Why not?" He pushed his hipster glasses up on his nose. "Your grades are fantastic. Your interest seems to be there. It's a diverse, excellent field."

"I took the career test with Mrs. Haberland," I began.

Rylander waved that thought aside. "Don't talk to me about those guidance office tests. Mine said I should be a florist. Don't go by a test. Don't even go by what Mrs. Haberland tells you. Go by your gut."

"Also . . ." *Ugh. How was I going to word this?* "I'm not sure if you know about, um, my family. But I don't know if someone like me would be welcomed in the, uh, scientific community."

He nodded. "Yes, I know about your ability. And that's exactly why you should think about joining the scientific community. You have a different perspective to offer. Have you thought about what colleges interest you?"

"A bit. I've been meaning to go on visits, but . . ." I paused, not even wanting to get into all the personal and familial complications that were filling up my time.

Rylander cocked his head to the side. An expression flitted across his face, perhaps pity. I realized that he probably knew a lot more about my situation than I figured. I had been all over the newspapers, after all. And the fact that I'd been bullied constantly probably wasn't a secret in the teachers' lounge.

"You know," he said softly, "I went to high school here, too. Not too long ago. And, this may shock you, but I wasn't exactly popular."

I gave a little chuckle.

"I had problems with bullies, problems fitting in." He looked at me with genuine concern. "But things will improve, Clare. I promise you."

I'd never had a teacher reach out to me like that before. Acknowledge that things were difficult for me here. And though his promise was empty — he couldn't guarantee things were going to get all sunny in my life anytime soon — I was grateful anyway.

"Thanks, Mr. Rylander."

He seemed pleased with my response. He patted his hands on his jeans, stood, and walked back toward his desk. His pep talk over, his voice switched from confidant mode back to serious-teacher mode. "Think more about your future. If you have any questions about careers in science, let me know." He wagged a finger at me. "And ignore those guidance tests."

I left the classroom thinking that Rylander's little speech came at a good time, since I'd been doing some soul searching myself. And I knew for sure what I wanted to do. Rylander's science idea was nice, but that wasn't exactly what I had in mind.

Perry, however, had me pegged correctly. And I *would* ignore the guidance test.

Because I doubted one of the options on it was Spider-Man: Sassy Girl Detective.

I took the long way home. No more cutting through the woods for me. I decided to stop at Mallory's house. She needed a friend right now. She might not want that person to be me, but I sure as hell was going to try.

There were no cars in the driveway, but both her parents worked, so I expected that. I rang the doorbell a couple times and waited. After what seemed like an eternity, Mallory opened the door, wearing black pajamas with little white skulls on them. Her hair stuck out at crazy angles.

"Sorry," I said. "Did I wake you up?"

"No." She opened the door wide, motioning for me to come in. "I took a mental health day. No showering allowed. Only lying on the couch and watching soap operas."

"I texted you a few times to see if you were okay. Are you still mad at me?"

"No, I don't have the energy to be." She slouched back on the couch and curled her legs up, making room for me. "Phone's up in my room. I've been down here all day."

I sat beside her. A sandwich with only one bite taken out of it lay abandoned on the coffee table. "So you heard about Sierra?" I asked softly.

She gave a little nod. Her eyes were focused on the television, a shell-shocked look to them. I glanced at the screen and saw it was only a detergent commercial.

In the awkward silence, I patted her knee, though the

gesture felt insignificant. She wasn't a five-year-old who'd just dropped her ice cream. But I didn't know what else to do.

"I'm all right," she said, possibly to make me feel better. "I'll be back at school tomorrow afternoon."

"That's good," I said.

She let out a long breath and drew in a deeper one. "It's weird. I feel like I already grieved for her. Like she died when she left." Her voice was flat. "And I shouldn't even be upset anyway. It wasn't like she was a great friend to me."

"It's only natural, Mallory." I'd been feeling like the air had been sucked out of my lungs all day and I'd never even known Sierra. Never even spoken to her. I could only imagine how Mallory felt.

I watched as her face turned red from the effort of fighting back tears. She brought her fists up to her eyes.

"You can let it out," I said.

She pulled her knees up and lowered her face to rest against them. Her voice was muffled as she spoke. "My parents both work so much and even when they're home, they're busy with their hobbies. The only reason I picked up photography was so my dad and I would have something to talk about. And school, well, you know how our school is. But I never minded how lonely I was during the day because I had Sierra waiting for me every afternoon." She lifted her face and wiped her tears away with the back of her hand. "In school, I'd focus on classes and my work, and then I'd come home to my only friend."

I felt a lump in my throat, relating to Mallory's loneliness. "It must have hurt a lot when she started ignoring you."

Mallory shrugged. "I should have expected it. She was always selfish. When we were little, she always got to pick what game we'd play. She always got to be Barbie and I had to be the sidekick. Even last year, for movie nights, she *had* to pick out the movie."

"Sounds bossy and self-centered," I said.

"It was half my fault because I let her do it. I never stood up for myself. When she said the homeschooling thing was done, I was so excited. Even though she was a year ahead and we wouldn't share any classes, I'd still at least have a friend in the building. But instead, she apparently made a new friend or a boyfriend. She didn't need me anymore."

Mallory paused to swallow hard. "She was my best friend and I was *nothing* to her." Her eyes turned wearily to me. "So why does it hurt? Why do I care?"

"Because you can't stop being a good person, even when your friend is being an ass. I know this from experience."

She smiled sincerely through her tears and I used my sleeve to wipe her cheeks.

"Thanks for listening."

"Thanks for letting me in," I replied. "You should know . . . I'm not Sierra. I'm not going to dump you for some other friend I deem better. And I told Brooke off that day after you left the lockers."

"You did?"

"Hell, yeah. I don't think any of it sunk in, but I tried."

She broke into a smile and then sighed. "Can we talk about something else? Something light and meaningless?"

"Sure. Whatever you want."

"Who did you choose?" She pulled herself up straight, and life returned to her eyes. "To ask to the dance?"

I didn't even want to think about the dance, much less talk about it, but Mallory needed this right now. "You know what might help you feel a little better?" I said. "If *you* went to the dance."

She shook her head. "No, no."

"It would take your mind off things."

"I have no one to go with."

"What about the person you wanted to ask before? The long shot, who was it?"

She grimaced. "I'd rather not say. I don't want you to feel weird."

"I won't," I insisted. "Just tell me."

She hesitated a moment. "It was your brother. I had such a crush on him when he went to our school, and I know he didn't go away to college, so I thought maybe . . ."

Perry? He was her big secret crush? I was surprised, though I shouldn't have been. Almost every girl at our school had crushed on him at some point. Ick.

"Why didn't you just tell me?" I asked.

"I didn't want you to think I was using you to get close to your brother. It's nothing like that. I want to be friends with you for you."

"I know." I shoved her jokingly. "I'm not sure if he'd go to the dance, though." I didn't want to share Perry's aversion to leaving the house, since that was personal, so instead I said, "He's sort of done with the whole high school scene, you know?"

"Oh, that's okay," Mallory said, nervously pulling a strand of hair across her face and turning the other way.

I was about to start listing other possible guys she could ask, but I knew her mind wasn't on that anymore. She was staring out the window and that dull haze had returned to her eyes. I followed her line of sight and saw Sierra's house through the glass.

"I want to know what happened," she said, with a catch in her voice. "I want to know who did this to her."

"You don't have any idea who she would have left with?"

She only shook her head.

A pat on the knee would do nothing to ease this sadness. Neither would a date with Perry. But one thing might help.

"We'll find out, Mallory," I said, staring with her out the window. "I promise I'm going to find out."

TWENTY-FIVE

MOM DRUMMED THE STEERING WHEEL NERVOUSLY while she waited for me to settle in. I dropped my book bag on the floor between my feet.

"Thanks for driving me to school." I snapped my seat belt into the buckle and adjusted it so it would stop strangling me.

"I'll pick you up this afternoon, too," Mom said, her voice tight.

I looked at her, confused. "But you like to be home in case we get business. Send Perry."

Her mouth turned down. "Perry's unreliable and I don't want you walking home anymore."

The news about Sierra Waldman's murder had hit our house like a bomb. Mom went on high alert, pacing the floors, checking and rechecking the locks before bed. Perry headed into his room and, from what I'd seen, hadn't come out. My heart went out to him. This had to be bringing back bad memories, and that was something he didn't need right now.

"Okay," I said. "But I don't want it to interfere with the business. I can get a ride from friends."

"I don't care about the business right now."

Starla Fern was normally as likely to say those words as she was to speak Latin backward. I gave her a sideways look.

"In fact," she said, drawing the words out slowly as she looked both ways at a stop sign, "I'm thinking of taking a little break. Thinking the family should go away for a while."

I stared at her. "What?"

"Until Sierra's killer is caught," she clarified, as if I didn't already know what had kicked off this overreaction.

"I can't miss school," I said.

"You can miss a few days."

"But what if the case isn't solved that quickly? What if it takes weeks? Months? I'm not going to repeat eleventh grade because of this, Mom."

Her jaw was set. "Maybe you should if it means keeping you safe."

I couldn't believe this was happening. I finally had a life outside of my house. I had friends. I had Justin and Gabriel. I had things to look forward to. The bonfire Friday night. Perhaps even the dance Saturday night. I was not going to scurry away and leave everything behind because of what happened to someone I didn't even know. Plus, I wanted to help the investigation, not hide from it.

But now I definitely couldn't tell Mom about my intentions.

"Sierra Waldman was killed," I said carefully. "One person. That doesn't mean we have a serial killer on our hands out there looking for his next victim. She got involved with the wrong person and ended up dead. It's terrible, but it has nothing to do with me."

"Victoria Happel's death this summer had nothing to do with you until you involved yourself."

"If I hadn't involved myself, Perry would be in prison right now."

"I'm not going to argue with you about this, Clare. You need to promise me you're going to stay away from this case, or we're packing up and leaving. I don't care about school or any plans you have. All I care about is you."

Her eyes were wild. I'd never seen her so panicked. I understood, though. After what went down this summer, she'd barely let me out of her sight for a month. And now she was scared. She didn't want to be in the position Tracy Waldman was in.

I'd told Mrs. Waldman I'd help. And I'd promised Mallory I'd find out the truth, too. But the only way I could salvage my life was to assure Mom that I wouldn't involve myself. And then decide which promise to break.

The car eased up to the curb in front of the school. I turned to face my mom. "If I promise not to investigate, we can stay?"

"Yes."

"What if the police ask for my help again?"

"This time, we'll say no," she said firmly.

"Okay. I'll stay out of it."

Mom sighed in relief, leaned over, and kissed the top of my head. I was always going to be her little girl. She would always worry and her first instinct was always going to be to overreact and overprotect me. That's just how she was. I grabbed my stuff and headed toward the front door of the school, sure of one thing.

If I wanted to stay in Eastport and hold on to my life as I knew it, I couldn't tell Mom about my secret admirer.

My teachers had apparently all conspired to give quizzes — planned and pop — on the same day. I aced Rylander's but wasn't as prepared for Mr. Frederick's and Mrs. Cotler's. I was mentally exhausted by the time the bell rang at the end of the last period.

The sounds of slamming lockers and simultaneous conversations filled the hall as I riffled through my stuff, pulling out the books and notebooks that needed to come home. Finally, I slung my backpack over my shoulder and joined the exiting crowd. Instead of heading toward the back door, I was among the stream of kids bottlenecked at the stairwell, all shuffling toward the front exit, where buses and cars idled.

Just as I was almost at the front doors, I felt something in my eye. I blinked rapidly, but the pain only worsened. Groaning, I turned around and staggered against the flow of traffic toward the closest bathroom. I pushed the door open, one hand over my closed eye, and rushed up to the mirror. I pulled down on my lower lid and saw the sucker. Eyelash. I got it out and sighed in relief as the irritation went away.

Only then did I realize I wasn't alone.

Kendra was in the corner, hovering over the last sink, using one of those rough brown paper towels to wipe smudged makeup from beneath her eyes. Her face was blotchy and red, as if she'd been crying.

I reached into my book bag and pulled a tissue from the little travel pack I always kept in there. "Here," I said, passing it to her. "That'll work better."

"Thanks," she said softly, refusing to meet my gaze.

The reason I knew how much it sucked to wipe away tears with a hard, cheap, school paper towel was because I'd done it myself. Quite a few times over the years, because of Kendra and her friends.

I wondered if she realized it.

"You all right?" I said, moving closer.

She turned away. "Just leave me alone."

I thought about the times I'd hidden in here, locked myself in a stall, hoping no one would come in and catch me crying quietly. But a small part of me had simultaneously wished someone *would* walk in. They'd ask me what was wrong. They'd care.

"You can tell me what's wrong if you want."

"Yeah, right." She looked up with her swollen eyes. "Why would you care? You hate me."

"I'm standing here talking to you after what you did to me at your party. That has to count for something."

"Brooke said you told her off."

I shrugged. "You two never wanted to be my friends. You wanted to use me as your circus monkey. That's not what friends do." I paused. "Friends also don't compete with each other. Go after their guys."

Kendra's mouth drew tight and she looked down at the dirty linoleum floor. So that's what the tears were for. Tiffany's betrayal.

"I don't have a date to the homecoming dance," she said.

"Don't go. Not everyone goes."

She rolled her eyes. "Kendra Kiger goes. I can't be voted princess if I don't go."

"What's that?"

"In the Homecoming Court. Two seniors are voted king and queen and two juniors are voted prince and princess."

I wondered how much of this pressure she was putting on herself and how much of it was coming from her mother. But to mention that would lead to telling Kendra about the vision I'd had in her house. And . . . that would be awkward.

I lifted myself up onto the counter and swung my legs as I talked. "There are plenty of guys still without dates."

"Yeah, they're either losers or Clare Fern holdouts."

I laughed.

"Seriously," she said, giving a little giggle herself. "Just ask one of them or put them both out of their misery."

"We're not talking about me right now," I said. "How about you go with a girlfriend? Go with Brooke."

"She's going with Jordan. They got back together at my party. Plus, my mother would freak out. I need to go with a hot guy. Homecoming King material. Brendan was perfect, but I was playing hard to get and waited too long to ask him. I never thought Tiffany would turn around and ask him behind my back."

I held my hands up in an *I told you so* kind of way.

"I know," Kendra said. "But she hated you. I didn't think she'd do something skeezy to a friend."

Suddenly, I remembered that my mother was sitting outside in the car, waiting for me.

"You'll think of someone. It'll all work out." I slid down off the counter. "But I've got to go. My ride's waiting." *And probably thinking I've been kidnapped by a serial killer at this point.*

"I'm going to stay here for a few more minutes," Kendra said, her eyes returning to the mirror. "I don't want anyone to see me like this."

I pulled open the heavy bathroom door and stepped into the quiet of the now deserted hallway. My sneakers squeaked on the waxed floor. A door closed somewhere behind me. Muffled conversation drifted up from downstairs.

I had almost reached the end of the hallway when I heard a sudden, quickening shuffle behind me. Then I was slammed against a locker. A forearm clamped like a vise on my neck, smushing my face against the cold metal.

A voice, hot in my ear, snarled, "You think you're *soooo* special, don't you, Clare?"

TWENTY-SIX

I STRAINED TO TURN MY HEAD AND FACE MY attacker. My struggling only made him laugh. My arms were pinned, but my feet were free and I calculated, aimed, and brought my heel down hard on his foot.

He yelped and stepped back, releasing me.

I brought my arms up defensively, then relaxed when I saw who it was. Cody Rowe. That useless moron. I wasn't afraid of him.

He narrowed his eyes and gave me one of his smarmy looks. "You're walking around here thinking you're hot shit," he said. "You think you're so special with your family of freaks. I had to pay cash money to get my car fixed, bitch." He pointed in my face. "My dad was pissed."

"Why are you telling me?" I glared defiantly up at him. "I had nothing to do with it."

He took a step toward me, closing the space between us. I pushed myself back against the locker, ignoring the pain of the dial against my spine. I'd always thought of Cody as all bark and no bite, but the menacing look in his eyes had me questioning that assumption. My heart sped up as I considered my possible moves. Cody was a huge guy, a football player. If I tried to get away, he'd toss me back as easily as if I were a doll.

I couldn't do this myself. I needed help. As he inched closer, his lips set in a sneer, I opened my mouth to scream.

"What's going on here?" a voice boomed from an open doorway.

Cody quickly stepped back and I let out a deep breath.

Mr. Frederick marched toward us. "The school has a zero tolerance policy for physical violence, Cody."

"It was no-no-nothing, Mr. Frederick," Cody stuttered, probably full of fear that he'd be suspended and miss Saturday's big football game. "We were just talkin'."

Frederick's eyes slid to mine, and I gave an almost imperceptible shake of my head. He got the message.

"Just your luck, Mr. Rowe," he said. "I happen to be supervising detention today. Come on in and join us." He made a shooing motion with his hand at me. "Move along, Clare." ·

Cody turned to follow Frederick, and I headed toward the exit. As we passed each other, Cody hissed under his breath, "I'm not done with you."

Mom was only mildly apoplectic by the time I got to the car. Rather than subject her to the truth, I told her I had to stay after to ask a teacher a few questions about an assignment. Then, just in case she decided to eavesdrop on my brain, I focused on a running list of assignments I had due in each class.

When we got home, I lumbered up the stairs, not in any mood to start my homework. I shrugged my backpack from my shoulders and tossed it on the hallway floor. As I passed Perry's room, I heard him talking to someone in a hushed voice. I paused and leaned up against the door.

"Come on," Perry said, frustration evident in his voice. "I need answers. I need to know how you came through. And why."

I threw open the door without knocking, surprising Perry, who was standing in the middle of his room. Alone.

"Who are you talking to?"

"I was *trying* to talk to Ashley."

"She's here?" I looked around the room. As if I could see her if she were.

"No." He sank down onto a chair. "I was trying to conjure her. Call her. Whatever."

"And it didn't work?"

"I don't know what I'm doing," he snapped. Though I knew he wasn't mad at me. He was mad that he didn't understand what was going on. "Usually, I have the connected person with me or I can go to a place connected with the spirit, but Ashley's a mystery. There has to be a reason she was able to break through. I just don't know what it is."

"Can I help?"

"No." He raised a hand to rub his forehead. "I'm done trying. If it happens again, it happens. I obviously have no control over it."

"Okay." He needed time to himself. I turned to leave. As I

reached the hallway, he called out, "By the way, you got a package. I found it on the porch and put it on your bed."

I sighed heavily. "Thanks." Probably more college stuff that I couldn't even begin to think about yet.

I trudged into my room, still filled with anger over Cody and with weirdness from how bad I felt for Kendra. Seeing her crying in the same bathroom I'd shed tears in was unnerving. I shouldn't have cared. I tried to harden my heart, but it didn't quite take.

All these thoughts quieted, though, as I approached my bed and saw the package. It was a large rectangular box. This was no college catalog.

I tore the brown packaging paper off and lifted the lid. White tissue paper covered whatever lay beneath. My heart started to pound. My first instinct was fear. It could be a dead rat or black roses. I lifted the tissue paper.

My breath caught in my throat.

It stared up at me from the box. Beautiful, yet menacing.

The green dress. The one I'd tried on in the store with Mallory.

Someone *had* been watching me through the store window.

And that someone *really* wanted me to have the dress.

I hurriedly covered the dress back up with tissue paper, closed the lid, and shoved the entire package under my bed. My feelings, however, could not be hidden as easily. What did this control freak think? That I would be flattered he bought the dress for me? That I would actually wear it?

Some girls might find behavior like that appealing. The adventure and excitement of a mystery and all that. But I didn't like it.

In fact, I thought it was time I did some stalking of my own.

I got down on my hands and knees and pulled the box back out from under my bed. Then I sat with it on my lap, closed my eyes, and concentrated. I let my fingertips roam over the box, the mailing label, and the packaging paper. To my surprise, a vision started to surface.

He'd never messed up before. I'd tried using my gift on his note, his card, his photo . . . He'd always been careful not to leave an imprint. I was so excited that the vision tremored and waned, and I had to force myself to calm down in order to bring it back. I took a deep breath. My fingers tingled. The vision was cloudy at first, then slowly became clear, like a nearsighted person would see as she put on her glasses.

I saw my house.

His eyes were glued to my front door as he stomped up the walkway. His footsteps were heavy, as if he were wearing boots. I wanted him to look down at his clothing. I needed some clue as to who he was.

He clomped up the porch steps, loud and brazen. Didn't he care if someone heard him? Was he like the worst stalker ever?

With each step, my worry increased. As soon as he let go of the box, the vision would be broken. I needed something, anything before he put it down. Why didn't my front door have a freaking mirror on it? That would be helpful right now!

Then I saw it. The front window. Maybe I'd be able to catch his reflection in the glass. I breathed deeply, working hard to hold on to the image as he reached a finger out and rang the doorbell.

Wait . . . he rang the doorbell? What kind of stalker does that?

Then, as he leaned down to place the package on the porch, I glimpsed a reflection in the windowpane. Not of him, but of his vehicle.

A UPS truck.

My stalker hadn't made a mistake. The only vision the package held for me was that of the deliveryman who'd left it on the porch.

As the UPS guy let go of the package, the image turned black. Like someone yanked the cord on the TV. I opened my eyes. That's all I was going to get. Nothing. I pushed the package off my lap and slammed my fists on the floor.

My eyes narrowed at the overturned box. There had to be more I could do. Maybe some research that wasn't of the paranormal variety. I pulled the package back onto my lap and squinted at the UPS label. Return addresses were required for these things, right?

But, apparently, they didn't have to be correct. He'd used 325 Main Street as his return address. The police station. Very funny.

I wasn't ready to give up, though. I could try the dress shop.

I looked up the phone number and called. It rang six times and I started to wonder if they were closed, but then a harried voice said, "Lorelei's."

I was startled by the sudden answer and the tone of her voice. "Um, yes, I was wondering if you could tell me who bought a particular dress —"

"I can't tell you who bought the dress you wanted," she interrupted, then prattled on like it was a practiced speech. "You should have bought it when you first saw it."

She ended the sentence with finality, like she was about to hang up. Great customer service at that place. I yelled, "Wait!"

The woman sighed audibly. I heard loud chatter and squeals in the background. She was obviously busy. "I can't give you any information on what girl bought your dress," she said, not bothering to hide her growing annoyance. "Just come pick out another one."

"It's not that," I said. "Someone bought a dress *for* me and sent it to me anonymously. I'd like to thank the person."

A snarky laugh blurted out of her. "Do you really think I'd remember who bought what? Listen, both Halloween and the Renaissance Fair are in two weeks. I have a dozen customers in here, all demanding my assistance. I can't help you."

I was left with a click and a dial tone, and no further ideas.

I sank down onto the bed, feeling defeated.

I remembered the words my stalker spoke on the phone when I asked who it was:

Good things come to those who wait.

Maybe it was all leading up to this. Maybe he or she

planned on revealing himself the night of the dance, and sending me the dress was their way of ensuring I went.

Well, I wasn't going to play that game.

No one controls me.

I'd find somewhere to donate the dress. And I'd stay home the night of the dance.

I sighed, depressed. I still hadn't solved the problem of deciding who to ask to the dance, but I'd liked having that option. I'd started to think that going might be fun. I figured I could always make a last-minute decision to go stag or with Mallory. But now that choice was taken away from me.

Then I had a thought that warmed my heart a little bit. *I* couldn't go to the dance, but that didn't mean I couldn't help some other people enjoy it.

I leapt out of bed and grabbed my phone. I loved this idea. I felt back in control of my life. Like if I focused on getting something done, I wouldn't be a victim. I'd take the power back.

I dialed Justin's cell and he picked right up. "Hey, Clare. Calling to profess your love?"

I snorted. "Calling to ask a favor."

"Yes, I can be there in five minutes to give you a full-body massage."

"It involves someone else."

"I don't want to give anyone else a full-body massage."

Justin's flirty banter had already put me in a better mood. I knew I was doing the right thing. I paced back and forth across the room as I began. "I'm not going to the dance."

He hesitated a moment, then asked, "Not with anyone or not with me?" I could almost picture him bracing for the answer.

"Not with anyone," I answered quickly.

He let out a deep breath. "Okay. So what do you need?"

"I have a friend who really wants to go to the dance. Correction: She needs to go to the dance. She's had a rough time lately and I think it would be good for her. But she doesn't have a date."

"So you're not going to the dance, but you want me to go with someone else?"

"Just as friends."

"Of course." He paused. "So who is it?"

"Mallory Neely," I blurted.

"I don't know. I've never even talked to her."

"That's okay. Once you get to know her, you'll get along great. She's different, in a cool 'I don't care what anyone thinks' kind of way."

"I'm not sure . . ." he said, though I could tell he was seriously considering it. If he really didn't want to, he'd have just said no.

"You'll have a good time. I promise."

"My buddies are all going to the dance, so I *did* want to go."

"I figured as much, Mr. Sociable."

He laughed. "Okay, tell her I'm in. But make sure she knows my heart belongs to you."

"Don't flatter yourself. She's not going to throw herself at you. She's not that kind of friend."

I hung up and bounced from foot to foot in excitement. I couldn't wait to tell Mallory the good news. But first, I had one other person to help. Not a friend, but someone who could use one.

I dialed Gabriel's number and he picked up, sounding out of breath.

"Did I catch you in the middle of a set of jumping jacks?" I asked sarcastically.

"I was almost out the door," Gabriel said. "I was coming over to see you."

"Oh yeah?" My heart did a little jig.

"I have something I want to show you. Can I stop by?"

"Sure. I have a favor to ask anyway."

"See you in five."

What had started out as a terrible afternoon was starting to look up. I darted over to my mirror to check myself out. Not too shabby. I slicked on some gloss and smacked my lips together, then ran my fingers through my curls. Better.

I dashed downstairs, and before long, Gabriel's Jeep pulled into the driveway. I stepped back from the window so he wouldn't see that I'd been waiting. I let a couple beats pass after he knocked on the front door, then opened it with a smile.

"Hey." He rushed in, a bundle of papers in his hand.

There was no return smile, no "accidental" brushing of my skin. His posture was straight and firm. All business.

"What's that?" I asked, motioning to the pile.

"This is what I wanted to show you." His face was set in rigid determination. "We're going to find out who your stalker is."

TWENTY-SEVEN

"SHH!" I PULLED GABRIEL BY THE ARM TOWARD THE bottom of the staircase. I heard the clanging of pots and pans, which meant that Mom was attempting to start dinner in the kitchen. I didn't need her overhearing the word *stalker* and going into commando-Mom mode.

"Wait here a sec," I whispered.

I darted over to the kitchen doorway and stuck my head in. "Mom, Gabriel's here. We're going to hang out upstairs for a bit, okay?"

She had her nose buried in a cookbook, her brow furrowed in confusion. "Keep your door open," she said without looking up.

"Yeah, okay," I agreed and then returned to Gabriel.

"Let's take this upstairs."

Perry's door was shut again. We headed into my room and I closed the door about ninety-nine percent of the way. But not all the way.

"You haven't told your mother?" Gabriel asked.

I led him away from the cracked door and into the center

of the room. "She went ballistic over Sierra's death. I had to promise I wouldn't help with the case or get involved at all."

"Or what?"

"Or we'd be leaving town until the killer was caught. Which could be never."

"So if she knew you had a stalker —"

"I'd either never be let out of my room or she'd find a way to get us into the Witness Protection Program."

He nodded, but said, "I still think she should know." Then he looked down at the papers in his hands. "And I really think you should read what I printed out."

"What is it?"

"Well, my father won't help me with this at all because he's too busy on the Sierra Waldman case and he said whoever's doing this to you hasn't broken any law. Yet. So I decided to look into it myself."

He laid the papers on my desk and motioned for me to sit in the chair.

But I didn't want to sit down. I didn't want to start thinking about the stalker again. "So what did you find?" I asked, standing.

"I did research and printed out all this stuff on stalker types and the psychology behind them."

I shook my head as he spoke. "I don't want to read that stuff. It'll just freak me out."

"Please?" His eyes were serious, full of concern. "It might help us figure out who it is."

"It won't." I slumped into the chair and leaned forward, elbows on my knees. "He's too good. He covers his tracks too well. I'm going to just ignore him and he'll lose interest."

Gabriel cocked his head to one side. "Has something else happened?"

I felt a thickness in my throat as I admitted, "He sent me a dress."

"What?" Gabriel blinked in confusion.

"It's a homecoming dress I tried on at the store with Mallory but didn't buy. I think the stalker wants me to go to the dance."

Anger flashed across his face. "So let's go. Bait him. We'll go together, be ready, and trap him."

"No. That would be giving him what he wants."

Gabriel paced the room, rubbing the back of his neck.

"I'm taking control of this by doing the opposite of what he wants," I insisted. "I'm staying home."

"Okay," Gabriel said, resigned. "Whatever you want to do." He stopped pacing and sagged against the wall, his shoulders slumped.

"Can we talk about something else?" I said. "How are things going with your mother?"

I was dying to know if he'd made his decision. Or at least which way he was leaning. Ever since the moment I found out he might be leaving, it'd always been in the back of my mind.

Gabriel shook his head. "I don't feel like talking about that right now."

I desperately wished I'd inherited my mother's gift. Even

though I chided her for eavesdropping on people's thoughts without their permission, I'd totally do that to Gabriel right now.

"What was the thing you wanted to talk to me about anyway?" he asked. "When you called?"

I sighed. I'd been excited before, but now I was all tangled up in multiple emotions again. "Since I can't go to the dance, I wanted to ask a favor for someone." I shifted in my seat. "Kendra waited too long and now there isn't anyone left that she'd like to ask. But I know she'd go with you. She just wouldn't bother asking you —"

"Because she knows I'd say no. Listen, dances aren't really my thing. I'd go with you, but that's it. I have no interest in taking anyone else. Especially someone like Kendra Kiger."

"You don't know her whole story, though."

"And you do?" he asked skeptically.

"I know enough. Things aren't as easy for her as I'd once assumed. Her mother's . . . well, I don't want to get into it, but it would really help her out if you'd go with her. As friends, you know. She wants to be eligible for the Homecoming Court and all that."

He grimaced. "I'd really rather not."

I stood and stepped closer to him, my hands clasped in front of me. "Please? For me?"

He met my gaze. "She wouldn't do it for you, you know."

"Well, I can feel superior for my good deed." I flashed him a smile. "How's that for a selfish reason?"

He reached out and softly stroked the side of my face.

"You're always more concerned about other people than yourself."

"But will you go?"

"Will you at least come to the bonfire Friday night?"

"If Mom lets me, yes."

"Okay, then I'll go to the dance with Kendra." He hesitated a beat and added, "If you sit with me and go over what I found out online."

I glared at the papers. Despite how much I wanted to stick my head in the sand and ignore the information, it couldn't hurt to hear him out. "Deal."

Gabriel sat in my desk chair and riffled through the papers on his lap. "There are different types of stalkers. I thought we could go through each kind and see if the profile fits someone you know."

I settled onto the edge of my bed, brought my legs up to my chest, and wrapped my arms around them. "Okay."

"The most common type is called intimate partner stalkers."

"What are they?"

"Exes who won't accept that the relationship is over." He raised an eyebrow.

"What?" I said.

"Justin?"

I stiffened. "No way."

"Just think for a minute."

"No. I won't even consider it. Next type."

Gabriel sighed and returned his eyes to the papers. "Well, there are celebrity stalkers and political stalkers."

"Not me."

"Yeah." He stuck that page on the bottom of the pile and held the next one up. "There are also vengeful stalkers."

Dread settled into my stomach. "Sounds scary."

"They're mainly looking to get revenge. Anyone have a grudge with you?"

"Yeah, there's a line. Tiffany's at the head of it."

He considered that for a moment. "The research says that most stalkers are male."

"But only most, not all."

"True," he conceded. "So Tiffany's still a suspect."

"Okay, next?"

"The last one is the creepiest." He paused, as if he didn't want to read it.

"Go on," I said. "Just read it." Now that we'd begun, I just wanted to get it all out there. Get it over with.

"Some websites call them love obsession stalkers. Some call them erotomaniacs."

"Eww."

"But most," he continued, "call them delusional stalkers."

"Aren't all stalkers delusional in one way or another?"

"Yeah, but these guys are very dangerous. They believe they are in love with their victims and that they're destined to be together."

A foreboding feeling cinched my chest as Gabriel went on.

"They often have a whole fantasy world in their head of how their relationship is going to go. Their perception is distorted. So when they try to bring that fantasy to fruition and the victim doesn't return the affection . . ."

"What?" I asked, my throat tightening with anticipation.

"The stalker may become violent or even deadly."

Lovely. Just lovely.

"And who fits that profile?" My throat was so dry, I could barely push out the words.

"That's the problem," Gabriel said. "It could be anyone. Someone who knows you very well. Someone you met once. Or someone who noticed you, but you've never even seen."

Well, that narrowed down the list of suspects.

To the whole world.

TWENTY-EIGHT

I SPENT MOST OF MY ENERGY THURSDAY TRYING *not* to think. When worried feelings about Gabriel's leaving surfaced, I ate to bury them again. When thoughts about Sierra's death echoed in my head, I focused on class and homework to shut them up. And when my mind turned to the person who was obsessed with me, I did everything in my power to redirect. I felt as if just thinking about the stalker was giving the person what he or she wanted. My attention. My feelings. Whether positive or negative.

I started to see suspects everywhere. A boy who bumped into me in line in the cafeteria. The postal carrier who stared one second too long when handing me the mail.

Sierra Waldman's cause of death had been released. Strangulation. The police were running down tons of leads in the case, from sex offenders in the area to rumors of gambling debts Sierra's father owed. But every time I started to think about how I could help, my heart sank as I remembered there was nothing I could do. Despite how obligated I felt to use my gift, Mom kept my hands tied.

I used loud sound — music, television, movies — to quiet all these thoughts. Mom had gotten a big order for her dresses, so she'd been busy in her sewing room. I was thankful for that, at least.

By Friday, I was starting to feel a little better. I hadn't heard anything else from my stalker, so perhaps Operation Ignore would work after all. School had been relatively drama free. Mallory was delighted to have a date for her very first dance, however platonic it was. Kendra needed a little nudging, not wanting to accept a "charity date" from me at first. But they were both pretty happy, and doing something good for them warmed the cockles of my little black heart.

It was finally bonfire night and Mom had agreed to let me go as long as I was with a group. Since I was boycotting tomorrow night's dance and I'd rather stab myself in the eye with a pen than go to tomorrow's football game, I was excited to at least partake in this small part of homecoming weekend. Like I was a regular girl in high school.

I sat on the couch, waiting for my ride. The bonfire was on Town Beach, close enough to walk, but Mom didn't like that idea, and Mallory was pumped to drive anyway. Mallory's parents had bought her a car so she could be more independent. Mallory had said it was more of a *please get out of your depression so we can get back to our regular lives* bribe, but it worked. Mallory with her car was like a girl with her first crush; she wanted to be with it all the time. But at least it lifted her spirits and got her thinking about something other than Sierra.

The house was quiet. Perry was playing video games in

his room with his headphones on. Mom was in the back room working on her dresses. I'd already said good-bye to her. Now I just needed Mallory to get her butt here already. The silence was driving me nuts. Every little sound startled me. A sudden whir of the sewing machine. The click of the furnace turning on in the basement.

I needed to get out of there. Be with a big group of people. Laugh, flirt, gossip. Do normal things. I chugged a Diet Coke and stared out the window.

Just when I thought I was about to peel out of my skin, Mallory's bright yellow compact slid into the driveway. I'd never seen a car so small and so garish, but Mallory didn't care. She didn't even mind that it was like eight years old. It was all hers and it was freedom. That's all that mattered to her. And to me, as I bolted down the walkway and pulled open the passenger-side door.

"Why are you so late?" I asked, the words sounding much whinier than I intended.

Mallory rolled her eyes, her head, and her shoulders in one big annoyed movement. "My parents descended on me like the demon spawn of Oprah and Dr. Phil."

"For what?"

"To make sure I'm all right. You know, with the whole Sierra thing. Apparently, my mom got her hands on some book about teens dealing with grief, and they're all worried I'm going to off myself or something."

Mallory pulled into the line of traffic as casually as she mentioned death and suicide.

I stared at her. "*Are* you all right?"

"I'm as good as I'm going to get for right now. Grief doesn't disappear overnight. It's going to take some time. They need to understand that."

"Parents worry." I shrugged. "That's their job."

"They complained that I wasn't opening up to them, but it's hard to open up when it's more of an interrogation than a real conversation. I felt like any moment they were going to lock me in a broom closet with a heat lamp and a lie detector."

I chuckled. "Imagine what it's like living with a telepath for a mother. I have to focus on mundane things or stuff she hates, like zombies, when I think she's trying to sneak a peek inside my brain."

Mallory let out a little laugh-snort. "Yeah, I guess you have it harder. But what's cool about your mom is that she's around when you need her. My parents only want to have these so-called important talks when it's convenient for them. The day I stayed home from school, they both went to work, leaving me alone all day. But now tonight, because Mom read a stupid book, they decided to have this big talk. I told them I had places to go, people to see, but they said this talk was important and had to happen now. You know why? Because they had time for me now."

There were no street spots, so Mallory slid into a spot in the parking lot beside the beach. The lot was full, and crowds of people milled about, sipping colored drinks from clear water bottles.

"Well, we both escaped and we're here now," I said. "Let's have fun."

"Deal." Mallory turned off the ignition and pocketed the keys.

I hoped venting for a few minutes had made her load lighter and that she'd be able to loosen up and enjoy the night.

I left my coat in the car because I knew the fire would be warm. But as we walked through the lot, I cinched my sweater tighter around me against the bitter breeze swooping in off the ocean.

"Wow, look at that," Mallory said as we stepped onto the hard-packed sand.

The bonfire in the distance was raging high into the air, flames licking at the night sky. A sea of people in red crowded around it. I looked at Mallory's black hoodie and my gray sweater and realized we'd forgotten to wear the school colors. Oh, well. There was always my hair.

We walked briskly toward the fire, passing clumps of current students, alumni who were home from college, and townies who got into the football spirit a little too much, if you ask me. A few old guys sat in beach chairs, sharing stories about when they were on the team and all those great plays that I'm sure have been exaggerated in their minds over the years. A couple cops stood sentinel to make sure the fire or the crowd didn't get out of control.

By the time we reached the center of it all, the band had packed up their instruments, and the cheerleaders and football players were mixing about. We'd missed the pep rally. But that was fine by me. I didn't even know who we were playing against in the big game. Though I'd guess their mascot was a bear of some kind because the football team kept tossing stuffed teddy bears into the fire.

"So what do we do now?" Mallory asked. "I've never come to this before."

"Me neither," I admitted. "We missed the rah-rah, so I guess we just hang out and talk with people?"

I scanned the crowd for friendly faces, but everyone looked alike in the semidark. Everyone wore red Eastport shirts or sweatshirts. As the flames danced, orange shadows morphed the faces in the crowd. I wouldn't know anyone until they were up close.

The energy was contagious. Now and then someone would just roar, "EASTPORT!" and everyone would cheer in response. I couldn't get into the whole sports thing. But I was enjoying the fresh air, the distraction from stalker-thoughts, and being out of the house and away from Mom's worrying and Perry's gloom.

Someone tossed a fresh plank of wood on the fire. Smoke and ashes billowed out toward the crowd. We jumped back, coughing and waving our hands in front of our faces. After a moment, the fire consumed the new timber and we all inched forward again, hands reached out for warmth. I stared at the dancing flames, relishing the heat on my face.

"Clare."

My head snapped up. I thought I heard someone say my name, in almost a whisper. Just one little innocent word, but it was said with almost teasing venom. My nerves prickled as I felt the now familiar sensation of being watched.

I looked around, but no one stood out. No one was looking directly at me.

I leaned against Mallory. "Did you hear that?"

"What?" Mallory yelled over the noise.

"Someone passed by and said my name."

She shrugged and stuffed her hands in her pockets. Her eyes were mesmerized by the fire.

I could have imagined it. There were a million conversations going on at once, and people were streaming by constantly. Heck, my name could have even come up in one of those conversations. Or a passing person said something that sounded like *Clare* . . .

Bear. Yeah, the other team. We were burning bears tonight.

Suddenly, that Diet Coke I'd chugged didn't seem like the greatest idea. I'd have to make a visit to the porta-potties to pee. A Bud Light can lay in the sand by our feet. I made a mental note to use that as a marker so I could find our spot again.

I looked at Mallory, who was still lost in the flames, and said, "I'll be back in a few. Wait for me."

I scrambled through the sand and the crowd toward the bathrooms. Some guy ran by with no shirt on, a big red *E* painted on his chest. I finally reached my destination and, of course, there was a line. I stuffed my hands in my pockets and watched the bonfire from a distance. It was beautiful, really. Long flames snapped up, like arms trying to steal the stars. Orange embers flitted through the air like fireflies.

Minutes later, I made my way back to the bonfire. I pushed through the throngs of people, eventually finding the beer can, still half buried in the sand.

But Mallory was gone.

TWENTY-NINE

THE BONFIRE WAS TOO HOT TO STAND TOO CLOSE, but I'd slowly built up a tolerance to the heat, so if I backed away from it, the night air seemed too cold. So I did this dance. Two steps forward, two steps back, to keep comfortable while I waited for Mallory to return. I didn't know where she would have gone. I told her I'd only be a minute.

"Hey!" a bubbly voice said as an arm draped around my shoulder.

It was Kendra, her hair pulled up into a high ponytail. She sipped from something in a brown paper bag.

"Have you seen Mallory?" I asked.

"No." Kendra frowned and pulled her arm back, but knew better than to add her usual insulting statement about my friend.

"She was here just a few minutes ago but now —"

"Is Gabriel around?" Kendra interrupted.

"I haven't seen him yet," I said. I was surprised, too. He'd been so insistent on wanting to know "for sure" if I was coming to this or not. He even wanted to know what time and all the specifics.

"I need to talk to him about what time we're going to the dance," Kendra said. "I called out to him in the hallway at school, but he didn't hear me."

Or pretended not to hear, I thought.

"I'll tell him," I said.

She put a hand on her hip and sighed. "I know you're, like, forcing him to do this and everything, but he can at least pretend he's not completely disgusted by me."

"He's not," I said. "Not at all. He's just going through some family stuff right now. He has a lot on his plate."

"There you are." Justin skidded up to me and gave me a little bump with his hip.

"Speaking of an overflowing plate," Kendra said to me, her eyebrows raised, before walking off.

Justin looked at me in confusion.

"Ignore her," I said.

"I always do," he replied. His eyes lit back up as he changed the subject. "So, your first bonfire! How do you like it?"

"It's fun," I said. "Though I lost my date."

His gaze dropped down.

"Mallory," I said, clarifying.

He raised his finger in the air. "Ah, I forgot! I was just talking to her a minute ago. I went up to introduce myself. You know, since we're going to the dance together and all."

"Thanks again, by the way."

"It's no problem. She's real nice."

He seemed sincere and I was glad. I really wanted Mallory to have a good time, especially after what she'd been through.

I knew I could count on Justin to treat her well. He was never one to care whether a person was popular or not. Exhibit A . . . me.

"So where's Mallory now?" I asked.

"She said she was going back to the car for a coat or something."

"That's not a bad idea," I said, realizing I was hugging myself for warmth. "I'm going to catch up with her to get mine, too."

"I'll save you a cozy spot by the fire," he called out.

I jogged toward the lot, my sneakers scratching against the grains of sand as my legs pumped. I wanted to catch up to Mallory before she reached the car so I wouldn't have to make her double back. The sounds of the crowd and the roaring fire dimmed behind me until all I heard was my heavy breathing, my shoes pounding the sand, and . . . something else.

I paused, thinking I heard footsteps matching mine. I looked around, but saw only darkness. The fire was too far behind me, and the streetlamp of the parking lot too far ahead. I ran faster, kicking up sand as I sped along.

I caught up to Mallory, who was walking at a leisurely pace, in the parking lot. She spun around at the sound of my ragged breathing.

"Justin told me you were going to get your coat," I said. I bent over a bit to catch my breath. "I want mine, too."

"You ran all the way here?" Mallory said, surprised.

"Yeah." I straightened and wiped my forehead with the back of my hand. "After that, I'm not even cold anymore."

Mallory threw her head back in laughter as we reached the car. She popped the trunk and leaned in to grab her jacket.

"Mine's in the backseat," I said, waiting for her at the door. "It's unlocked."

I opened the door and squinted as the interior light went on. I reached in and grabbed my brown coat, then pulled it out. But something else came with it.

"Whoops," I said, glancing at the large manila envelope that had fallen to the ground. I bent down to grab it, but picked it up by the wrong end. Its contents spilled onto the asphalt.

"Oh, crap. I'm sorry, Mallory. I'll pick all this up."

"Pick what up?" her muffled voice responded.

I was glad she was busy riffling around in the trunk and hadn't seen the mess I made. I hoped this wasn't anything important.

My heart sank as I realized they were photographs. She'd probably agonized over getting all the right angles and lighting and all that stuff photographers care about and I'd gotten them all dirty.

I got down on my hands and knees, ready to carefully pile them back up and return them to the envelope, when the first one caught my eye.

It was me. A color photo of me trudging down the hill by the back of the school.

I picked up another. Me entering the woods.

Me in the woods.

Me walking down the street.

Me looking over my shoulder, fear etched on my face.

Mallory shut the trunk and stuffed her arms into her coat sleeves. "What are you doing on the ground?"

I stood in one swift motion and faced her. "Are these yours?"

She shook her head, looking at the mess on the ground. "What are they?"

"They're pictures of me."

Her eyes widened. I held out the photo I clutched in my hand.

She took it, shaking her head as her eyes scanned it. "This isn't mine."

"Then why were they in your car?"

Mallory's worried eyes turned suddenly defiant. Her chin jutted out and her hands gripped her hips. "My car was unlocked, Clare."

I didn't know what to believe. Had someone put the pictures in her car to frame her? Or maybe I kept believing her excuses because I didn't *want* her to be guilty. Maybe she'd been playing me all along. Everything kept circling back to her again and again.

Mallory's eyes suddenly flicked from mine to somewhere behind me, and narrowed.

"Someone's watching us," she said in a low voice.

I turned around as I heard the distinct drag of a footstep. You can't move in a beach parking lot without making noise. All the sand and gravel tracked over the pavement makes that impossible. But someone was trying to back slowly away from us. Someone disappointed that he'd been caught.

"Come out!" I yelled.

I was so sick of this. Sick of the notes. The photographs. Suspecting everyone. Not trusting anyone. I wanted it to end.

My rising anger and frustration infused me with nerve. I marched through the lot, peeking behind each car I passed, screaming the whole way.

"Come on, coward! I know you put the pictures in the car!

"You want me so bad? Here I am!

"Face me!"

Mallory scurried along behind me, her face aghast at my display.

I banged my fist on the hood of a rusty old truck. "Let's end this now!"

I turned a corner to the next aisle and found him huddled down. My feet skidded to a stop. Mallory caught up quickly and gasped.

"Cody?" Mallory said behind the hand she held over her mouth in surprise.

Cody stood slowly and straightened to his full height. "Yeah, it was me." He puffed his chest out and stepped toward me, eyes flashing with disdain. "What are you gonna do about it?"

"Why?" I said, my mind still processing what was happening. "Why would you go through all this trouble?"

"It was Tiffany's idea," he said. "She noticed you were happy with your new freak friend." He jerked his chin in

Mallory's direction. "Tiff wanted to make your life a little more exciting. You should thank her."

I wanted to hit something. I wanted to throw up. Every time I thought Tiffany couldn't sink any lower, she proved me wrong. Even though Cody was standing there, confessing, I still couldn't believe it.

"You guys did all this just to . . . break Mallory and me up?"

He shrugged. That one movement had never seemed so cold and heartless on any other person before.

"Tiffany likes to play with you." His voice was full of condescension. "You're like her little toy."

My fingernails bit into my palms as I squeezed my fists tight. I hated being manipulated. Tiffany had pulled my strings and I'd danced. I filled with anger, desperate to lash out. "You would know," I said to Cody. "You're her favorite toy of all."

His face reddened and he took a long stride toward me. "What's that?"

My eyes gleamed with the knowledge that I'd hit him in his weak spot. "Tiffany gives you all these orders and you do every . . . single . . . thing she asks. And what do you get in return? Did she ask your ugly ass to the dance? Hell, no. She asked Brendan."

Cody's body tensed, the veins in his neck bulging, but I continued. Once the words started, I couldn't stop them.

"Did you really think you'd ever have a chance with her?" A laugh escaped from my mouth. "She has no feelings for you and never will. She uses you. She strings you along. Everyone knows it. Everyone sees it. They laugh about it behind your back. I bet *she* even laughs about it. How pathetic you are. Her shadow. Her little puppy dog, always nipping at her heels, begging for scraps of attention."

A sudden storm of anger erupted from Cody. He leapt forward, grabbing my arms and pinning them to my sides. He pushed me back against a truck. I yelped in pain as my head hit metal.

Mallory yelled, "Hey, stop!" and pulled at Cody's sleeve. He shrugged her off like she was a fly. Just a light push and Mallory was stumbling backward.

Cody turned his attention back to me. His entire body was pressed against me, so hard it hurt to breathe. I struggled uselessly to free my arms. His breath smelled sour and rotten, and I twisted my head to the side to try to escape from the scent and sight of him.

Time seemed to be going in slow motion. I heard a vague rushing sound. I closed my eyes, hoping Mallory would be stronger this time.

And suddenly, Cody was torn away from me. The force of it made me stagger a few steps. Mallory caught me in her arms and pulled me back with her. I didn't understand what was going on. If I was with her, who was rolling on the ground with Cody?

My eyes adjusted as Mallory's grip tightened on my forearm. It was Gabriel. Pounding the living hell out of Cody. Gabriel was straddling him, and he held Cody's shirt bunched up in one hand as the other rained down with punch after punch. Each one accentuated by a word.

"Never!

"Touch!

"Her!

"Again!"

After a few moments of standing frozen, staring at the almost surreal sight before me, I jumped into action.

"Gabriel," I called, moving toward him.

He stopped at the sound of my voice. He stood and backed up, his eyes never leaving Cody's crumpled frame. Blood trickled from Gabriel's knuckles, but I didn't know if it was his or Cody's since Cody had a good amount leaking out of his nose. Cody rolled to the side, cradling his arm and groaning.

"My arm," he moaned. "You broke my arm."

"Consider yourself lucky," Gabriel seethed, his face darkened in anger. He leaned over Cody one last time, his fists opening and closing. "If you even *look* at Clare again . . . I'll do much worse."

THIRTY

THERE WAS NO SECRET ADMIRER.

There was no stalker.

It was just another one of Tiffany's little plans to ruin my life. Just another prank to fill her time.

The truth hadn't even really settled in until I'd spoken it out loud to Gabriel last night, as he washed his bloodied hand in the seawater. He'd already known. He'd been watching all night, from a distance. He had a feeling the stalker was going to make a move at the bonfire. That's why he wanted to know when I was getting there, who I was going with, and all the other details. He wanted to be there, waiting. To protect me. To put an end to this.

And now it was over, and my emotions bounced all over the place like a rubber ball. I felt stupid for letting Tiffany get to me again. I felt angry for all the time and energy I'd wasted worrying about some obsessed person who'd never existed.

But then, after I got all that out of my system, my mind settled, and I was happy. There was no reason for me to be afraid. I was free.

Free to go anywhere I wanted.

Now I leaned closer to the mirror, applying eyeliner. I'd styled my mass of curls into a loose upsweep and left a few ringlets cascading down here and there. For all the time it took me, it looked very carefree. I liked that, though. And if there was ever a time to put a little more effort into your hair and makeup, it was for something like this.

A homecoming dance.

I stepped over to my closet and opened the door to take a look in the full-length mirror. The green dress was beautiful. Simple and classy, yet clingy in the right places to give me curves where I barely had them.

Wearing the dress made me feel a little bit like I'd won in this whole scenario. Instead of bending to the will of my so-called stalker's wishes, now it seemed like I was rubbing Cody and Tiffany's noses in their failure. They'd tried to terrify me, to destroy my friendship with Mallory, and ruin my life. Sure, they'd succeeded in scaring me here or there, but the rest of their plan had gone bust. So I'd wear the dress. I'd wear it proudly. I might even thank Cody for dropping the cash.

I slipped into a pair of strappy heels, grabbed my little white purse, and headed into the hallway. Perry's door was open, so I peeked my head in.

"Whatcha doin'?" I asked lightheartedly, hoping the tone would rub off on him.

He was bent over his laptop, staring at the screen while gnawing on his thumbnail. "Just trying again. It's bothering me."

I stepped into his room. "What is?"

"Ashley," he said, his eyes never leaving the screen. "I just can't figure it out. She said she was famous, but if she was she'd be Googleable. It doesn't make any sense. She's somehow related to the Sierra Waldman thing. I know it." His fingers hovered over the keys like it was a Ouija board that was going to start speaking to him. "But I'm missing something."

Guess I wasn't the only Fern with a growing sense of responsibility. "Why are you even looking into it? What are you trying to be — Perry Fern, Sassy Boy Detective?"

He smirked and glanced up at me like he was about to snap off a snarky retort, but then stopped. With a surprised little smile, he said, "You're going to homecoming? Good for you. Who did you ask?"

"I'm going alone."

"Ah," he said. "You waited too long."

I shuffled my feet and fiddled with my purse, not wanting to get into the details. "Something like that."

If I told him I'd set up Gabriel and Justin with other dates, he'd want to know why. Then I'd have to tell him it was because I'd been scared to go to the dance because I thought I had a dangerous stalker. At which point he'd get angry that I didn't keep him in the loop. And he'd realize it was because I didn't want to burden him with it and he'd feel like a failure as a brother. And when he found out the whole stalker thing was orchestrated by Tiffany, he'd feel even guiltier. He was the one who threw gasoline on her hellfire last year when they hooked up and he blew her off after.

So I kept quiet.

"What are you doing tonight?" I asked.

"Shooting zombies." He motioned toward his video game controller. "Maybe I'll call Nate, see if he wants to join in."

"Is he coming home again?" I said, one hand on my hip. "Does he even go back to college every Sunday night or does he just pretend that's what he does and he's really skulking around town?"

I was joking, but Perry's face turned serious. "He comes home because he's worried about his best friend, the shut-in. I'm ruining his life on top of mine."

My heart cinched. I actually felt physical pain inside my chest at the sight of my brother like this. "When was the last time you tried leaving the house?"

"Don't ask."

Mom's footsteps on the stairs caused his eyes to widen, and he motioned for me to leave. I entered the hallway as she reached the landing, carrying a laundry basket. At the sight of me, she put the basket down and clasped her hands together.

Before she could start, I said, "I know, I know. I'm going with a group. I'll be in a gymnasium with hundreds of other people."

Mom frowned. "I wasn't going to nag you. I was going to say you look absolutely dazzling."

She stepped closer and fingered a ringlet of my hair. "I probably overreacted to Sierra Waldman's death," she said softly.

I arched an eyebrow. "Ya think?"

"Don't be a smart-ass, dear, just let your mother apologize. I'm still not letting you work with the police at all." She paused and smiled sheepishly. "But I might have been a little overboard with all that talk about leaving town. Thanks for putting up with me."

I didn't blame her. As much as I resented her sometimes controlling, overprotective, mother-lion shtick, I understood it. I felt a twinge of guilt for having hid the stalker thing from her, but it had all worked out for the best. She'd have moved us somewhere else and listened in on my thoughts constantly until she drove herself insane. And for what? There hadn't been a real stalker after all.

I leaned over, two inches taller than her in my heels, and kissed the top of her head. "I love you, Mom."

She looked up at me, all glassy-eyed with gratefulness, and I was reminded how one seemingly insignificant affectionate act from me could mean the world to her. I vowed to do it more often.

A horn beeped outside.

"That's my ride."

Mom nodded, still all smiles from our little moment, and gave me one last squeeze. I carefully descended the staircase, unsure of my balance in my new shoes, my hand tightly gripping the railing.

I took the porch steps as carefully as I'd taken the stairs. Justin and Mallory waved from the front of the car. I hadn't felt weird earlier when Mallory offered to drive me. After all, they weren't on a real date. But now, sliding into the backseat, I felt a little uncomfortable being the third wheel in her hoop ride. Like I was interrupting something.

I laid my purse on the seat next to me and buckled my

belt. "You guys look great," I said, though I hadn't really gotten a good look yet.

Justin glanced over his shoulder. "You, too."

"I'm glad you ended up coming," Mallory said, carefully backing out of the driveway. "It all worked out."

I was actually kind of excited to go to the dance dateless and just have a good time. I shelved any romantic thoughts about Justin and Gabriel, any vengeful thoughts about Tiffany and Cody, and my desire to investigate the Waldman case. I wanted just one night of mindless, harmless, high school fun.

After five more minutes of awkward small talk, Mallory eased the car into a spot toward the back of the packed school parking lot. I peeled myself off the seat, closed the door, and rearranged the hem of my dress. A few hand-holding couples were making their way through the dimly lit lot toward the open doors of the school gym.

Mallory came around from the driver's side, wearing that indigo dress from Lorelei's. Her hair was pinned up, with only the one blue streak hanging straight down and matching the hue of her dress perfectly.

"Damn," I said. "You look fantastic."

"Shut up," Mallory said, blushing.

"No, you do. Am I right, Justin?"

Justin had been staring at me, but now he turned to Mallory and nodded eagerly. "Clare's right. You really do."

Justin didn't look half bad himself. His father was the mayor, so he had to dress up for town events now and then. But even though I'd seen him like this before, that didn't take anything away from how handsome he looked in his dark gray suit with an already loosened blue tie.

"Shall we?" he asked, holding both arms out. Mallory took one, giggling, while I took the other.

I'd never been to homecoming before and was expecting to see an empty dance floor and nervous packs of boys and girls lining the perimeter, wringing their hands. Wrong.

The gym floor was a sea of bodies in motion, feet shuffling, hips swaying. More people were dancing than standing. Since it was mid-October, they'd gone with a Halloween theme: *Gettin' Witchy With It.* I'd call it tacky, but it kind of felt like home. Fake cobwebs were strewn here and there. Lamps with black-light bulbs were strategically placed near glow-in-the-dark decorations. A full moon hung from the ceiling, and a smoke machine pumped out fog from the corner. Couples could get their photos taken before a backdrop of a graveyard.

I pointed toward the photographer. "You guys should do that now before there's a line."

"No, no, we don't have to," Mallory said, though I knew she probably wanted to. It was her first homecoming, too.

"Of course we do," Justin piped up. "I'll drag you over there if I have to."

He gave my hand a light squeeze as he led Mallory away. I smiled widely. I couldn't have been happier about how the night was going. Justin was being so cool about everything. Mallory was having fun. Maybe I should start having some fun, too.

I worked my way through the crowd, searching for Gabriel, but didn't find him. I glanced at the groups of kids moving to the music on the dance floor, some more awkwardly than others. The music wasn't really my type, kind of soulless, but good for dancing. I tentatively joined a circle of other junior girls, wondering how this was going to go, but before I knew it, I was jumping up and down, yelling out the lyrics with them.

After a couple songs, my neck was damp with sweat and my feet were killing me. I really should have worn heels that were already broken in. I wandered away from my little dance crew and headed toward the hallway where the closest water fountain was, hoping to quench my suddenly overpowering thirst. But as I reached the door and looked through the little glass window, what I saw constricted my throat so tightly I could barely swallow.

THIRTY-ONE

KENDRA WAS ON GABRIEL LIKE A PREDATOR ON A slab of meat.

For each inch he backed away from her, she stepped a foot closer, until his back hit the hallway wall. Kendra had one hand at the nape of his neck and with the other, her fingers stepped up his tie, slowly, until they reached his face. I couldn't hear what she was saying, only the sexy intonation she was putting in her voice. She trailed a finger along his lower lip and leaned in for a kiss.

My heart pounded. Was I watching history repeat itself? Memories of Tiffany's seduction of Justin were bad enough. I couldn't watch it happen again.

Gabriel turned his face away, blocking Kendra.

But she wouldn't be so easily deterred. She murmured something in a low tone, leaned her body up against his, and pressed her lips to his now exposed neck. Then he put his hands on her.

But to push her away.

She stumbled back and gave him a throaty laugh. Like it was a game. Like he was playing hard to get.

He snapped, "What's wrong with you?" and marched down the hallway toward the classrooms and away from the gym. He didn't see my face in the window.

But Kendra did.

She turned back toward the gym, her mouth stretched in a sly smile, and stopped mid-stride when she saw me. I threw my weight against the door, so hard it hit the wall with a slam.

"What do you think you're doing?" I said.

Kendra crossed her arms. "Whatever, Clare. It's not like he's *yours*. If you wanted him, you would have taken him by now. You can't reserve him in case you decide you want him later."

She wasn't even slightly apologetic. I was incredulous. I wanted to bang my fists against the wall and scream. It took an inhuman amount of effort for me to say, in a controlled tone, "You were crying in the bathroom when Tiffany did this to you, and now you turn around and do the same thing to me?"

Kendra shrugged and stretched her fingers out to examine her manicure. "Tiff and I made up last night. We're cool now. I know you're new to this scene, Clare, but here's a tip. He's just a boy. Get over it and move on. You can't let boys get in the way of friends."

"But that's the problem," I said. "You have no idea what it means to be a friend."

I shook my head. Kendra, Tiffany, Brooke . . . they just didn't get it. Yeah, at first glance, that crew looked like fun. Parties every weekend. Sitting at the cool table in the cafeteria. All that. But it wasn't worth it. One day, friends. The next day, enemies. Lather, rinse, repeat.

"Don't come talking to me anymore," I said, and walked off. I'd given them a chance, like my mother made me. And they'd blown it.

I searched the sea of faces for my real friend and found Mallory easily enough by her dress. She stood in a back corner, her shoulders slouched forward, seething at a small circle of girls with their arms wrapped around each other.

"What's going on?" I asked when I got closer.

Mallory stepped aside and I saw. A small memorial had been set up for Sierra. An enlarged framed photo of her sat on an easel. Several flowers were strewn on the floor beneath it.

"They make me sick," Mallory said, staring defiantly at the crying girls. "They didn't know Sierra. They'd probably never even stooped so low as to talk to her. They're fake tears."

The girls had moved on from their mini-breakdown and rejoined a larger group on the dance floor. Within seconds, they were throwing their arms in the air and yelling, "Wooo," when their favorite song came on.

I frowned in disgust. "But why bother with the tears? What's the point?"

"Knowing someone who was killed gives them a chance at quasi-fame. A scary 'it could have been me' story to tell when they go away to college. A sad story for their application essays." Mallory straightened. "They're not mourning her. They're using her."

I nodded, knowing she was spot on. I turned away from the girls with revulsion and examined Mallory in her sadness. I wanted to open up. Tell her why it took so long for me to trust her. Explain how most of my experience with girls had resulted in ridicule and hurt, and I'd learned to block myself off. But I struggled with the words. Sarcastic one-liners came more naturally.

I cleared my throat, catching her attention. "Friendships don't come easy for me," I said, staring down at my clasped hands. "So I'm sorry if I kept you at a distance and didn't fully let you in at first. I've learned to expect the worst in people. And I don't trust easily. The only true friends I've ever had are my brother and his best friend." I looked up at Mallory. "But I'm glad I've got you now, too."

It felt good to be honest. To share something real. Something deep. And, whether Mallory realized it or not, it took a lot for me to say all that.

She took one last glance at Sierra's picture, then turned back to me. "You might be my *first* true friend."

We shared a quick hug, then turned back toward the dance floor. A slow song was playing now. Girls danced with their heads on their dates' chests. Many of them had ditched their heels, choosing to dance barefoot. The gym was steaming with body heat.

I felt myself flush with warmth as I saw Gabriel off to the side, scanning the crowd, looking for someone. His eyes found mine and locked on with an intense expression.

"I'm going to go, uh, get a drink," Mallory said, giving me a wink over her shoulder as Gabriel strode toward me.

He wore a black suit that worked so well with his dark hair and eyes. The crisp white shirt contrasted with the black tie. His usually unruly hair had been tamed by gel. As he strode over, several girls stopped to look at him. I wished I could make all the other people and the noise disappear. Like a wish come true, when he reached me and took my hand in his, the music and voices muted into the background.

"Dance with me," he said.

I let him lead me to the dance floor. His arm circled my waist, drawing me closer to him.

"I know Kendra threw herself at you," I began. "I'm so sorry for setting you up —"

"That's not important," he said, placing a finger on my lips. "Let's not waste another second talking about her."

I sucked in a deep breath, realizing what was going on. Why he looked so serious. He didn't want to waste any time because there wasn't much time left.

"You're going to New York, aren't you?" I said gently.

He gave me a long look and in that time I felt everything amplified. The fabric of his suit jacket on my arm. The muscles in his shoulders beneath my hands. The sweet smell of his breath. The warmth that coursed through me as his hands moved down to my lower back.

Finally, he spoke. "I've been all torn up inside over this decision. And part of me was dragging my feet because I was waiting on you."

"On me to what?"

He ignored my question. "I've made a few friends here, but I have more back home. I have one parent here, one there.

I have the beach here, the city there. It's all equal. The tipping point is you."

"That's not true. You have the hockey team and —"

"And I'm on the team back home. Honestly . . ." He cleared his throat and a tinge of red rose to his cheeks. "Without you, there's no reason for me to be in Eastport. I thought you realized this, and I've been waiting for you to make a decision. I didn't want to do this. But I'm running out of time here. So I have to do it."

"Do what?" I said through my tightened throat.

"Ask you." He stopped our slow, shuffling dance and looked directly into my eyes. "Clare. Give me a reason to stay."

THIRTY-TWO

THE SONG ENDED AND GABRIEL DROPPED HIS HANDS from my body. "Let me know tonight, all right?" he said. "Tell me to stay, to be with you . . . or let me go."

My arms remained in the air for a few moments after he walked away, like they were draped around a ghost's shoulders. I closed my eyes and inhaled deeply. If I chose Gabriel, he'd stay. If I chose Justin or procrastinated any longer, he'd leave. It wasn't an ultimatum, really, just Gabriel being honest, as usual.

I felt almost paralyzed. I stood in the center of the dance floor, all alone, surrounded by people living their own dramas while mine had come to a head. I told myself to move. Just walk, in any direction. I shuffled over to a table adorned with a banner that said CONGRATULATIONS.

I'd missed the whole coronation-of-the-court crap at the game today, but a pink poster on the table told me that Kendra hadn't won. Tiffany had. Reading the words, I felt nothing, since I didn't even know who was the lesser of the evils anymore. What did raise an eyebrow was Tiffany's guy. His name was Brenden, not Brendan. Not that I'd ever thought much about him, but I never realized that was how he spelled his name.

And then a thought occurred to me. A long shot, but worth making a quick call.

I pulled my cell out of my purse and scrolled down to Perry.

He picked up after a few rings. "Yeah?" I heard the sounds of gaming-related shotgun blasts in the background.

"Hey, I had a thought," I said.

"Don't hurt yourself doing that," he joked.

"What if Ashley isn't spelled the traditional way? We didn't search for her as A-S-H-L-E-I-G-H or A-S-H-L-E-A or A-S-H-L-E-E or —"

"Yeah, yeah, I get the point. I'll check it out later."

"Just do it now. It's a simple search."

"You're supposed to be dancing," Perry said. "And these zombies aren't going to shoot themselves."

I groaned and slipped the phone back into my purse.

Cody Rowe walked by, with one arm in a sling and the other around a tiny blond girl with an upturned nose who looked around like she owned the place. I didn't know her name, but recognized her. I'd seen the way the crowd opened for her as she walked down the freshman hall. She was a miniature Tiffany, waiting to inherit the crown. It never ended. When we graduated and Tiffany and Kendra were gone, this girl would slide right into their place. And after she was gone, there would be another.

"Everything okay?"

I looked to my left and found Rylander wearing his usual

shirt/tie/jeans ensemble. "Sure, Mr. Rylander. Everything's great."

He sauntered over, his hands in his back pockets. "It's a shame Cody Rowe couldn't play in the big game," he said.

My mind registered the sling. The damage Gabriel had done made Cody miss the most important game of the year.

Rylander continued, "Word is he tripped at the bonfire Friday night."

I couldn't help but smile as I said, "What a shame."

My eyes went to Rylander and he was smiling, too. "Thanks for your advice the other day, Mr. Rylander," I said.

"It's no problem, Clare. Now I must return to staking out the punch to ensure that it stays nonalcoholic." He winked and walked away.

My lightened mood would be short-lived, though, as I spied Tiffany striding purposefully toward me. Her hair was pinned in a complicated updo, and the two ringlets hanging down on each side shook as she stomped over. I planted my feet and balled my hands into fists at my sides, readying for battle.

"You know, that was really low," she snarled. "What you made your boy toy do to Cody. He might miss the rest of the season."

My mouth opened and closed like a fish gasping for water. "You're whining to me? Are you serious? After everything you did?"

"It was a little prank. Not a big deal. Gabriel's the one who turned it violent."

Yeah, like Cody pinning me to a car by my throat wasn't violent. I put my hands, palms up, into the air.

"Not a big deal?" I started in. "You stalked me for weeks over email, the phone, leaving stuff for me to find everywhere, following me day after day taking pictures —"

Tiffany cut me off. "What the hell are you talking about? All Cody did was follow you one afternoon on your way home from school. He snapped a bunch of pics and planted them in Mallory's car so you'd think she was a psychotic freakbag. Which I still think she is, by the way. So really I was doing you a favor."

"Wait. So you didn't send the flowers and the email or call me or send me this dress?"

Tiffany looked me up and down. "Are you high? Why would Cody or I drop money on a dress for you?"

I blinked rapidly, still processing. "So you're saying all you did was have Cody follow me once and take a few pictures and put them in Mallory's car."

"Um, yeah. Hello."

"Did he do more on his own?"

"And not brag to me about it after? Unlikely." A shadow passed over her face as something dawned on her. Her expression morphed from bitchy petulance to something like concern. "Cody did say something, though. I didn't think anything of it, but . . ."

"What?"

"When he was taking pictures of you walking home through the woods, he thought someone else was there."

"Who?"

"He didn't see anyone. But he felt like someone was watching him. And he heard noises. So he got all spooked and took off. I didn't think anything of it. Cody just babbles on and on to me. But maybe Mallory was stalking you after all."

"No, it's not her." I was sure of it.

"Well, then, it's someone," Tiffany said, already walking away.

I rubbed my temples as I sifted through the information. If Tiffany was telling the truth, then she and Cody had only planted the photos. The calls, emails, flowers, and dress were from someone else. And the photo stuck in my locker was, too. I knew it was different from the ones I found in Mallory's car. It was done well, for one. And it was black-and-white, professional-looking. The ones in Mallory's car were in color and amateurish.

Something else occurred to me. The note . . . the very first note in my locker. That came before Mallory and I had really even talked. Before Tiffany would have had any reason to want to break up our friendship.

Maybe Tiffany was telling the truth for once. Maybe there had been a stalker after all. I looked around the gym, at the crowd of faces and sweaty bodies in the dim light. Suddenly, I didn't feel as confident as when I'd first arrived.

My phone started buzzing in my purse and I pulled it out.

"What's up, Perry?" I said, though I didn't care so much about his little ghost problem anymore.

"I've got her," he said excitedly. "It's A-S-H-L-E-I-G-H. And you'll never believe what I found out."

THIRTY-THREE

OUT OF THE CORNER OF MY EYE, I SAW GABRIEL approaching. He was patting down his suit jacket with a confused look on his face.

"Hold on," I told Perry. I put my hand over the phone and asked Gabriel, "What's wrong?"

"I lost my cell phone. I swore I left it on the table over there, just for a second, while I poured myself a drink. But it's not there. It's not anywhere."

"I'll help you look for it in a few minutes," I said. "I'm talking to Perry."

Gabriel nodded and meandered away through the crowd.

"I'm back. Who was she?" I asked, pressing the cell phone harder against my ear as if that would bring the answers faster.

"Ashleigh Reed was a painter," Perry said.

"So she *was* famous, just like she said."

"Well, within a small art scene, yes. She'd been a child prodigy. Amazingly gifted. Her work started selling in galleries when she was only ten. She left the country at age eighteen to go to some fancy-pants art school in Paris."

Okay, so far nothing mind-blowing. "When did she die?"

"Her first semester in Paris. Five years ago." He paused. "She was strangled. They never caught who did it, as far as I can see."

"Just like Sierra Waldman," I said, in barely a whisper.

My fingers started to tremble as ideas clicked into place. Sierra and Ashleigh were both strangled. And both were extraordinarily talented, though in different mediums.

"There's something else they have in common," Perry was saying in my ear. "This is the big one."

I was almost too scared to ask. "What?"

"Guess what high school Ashleigh graduated from?"

"You're kidding."

"Says it right here in the article. Eastport High in Eastport, Massachusetts."

I felt stunned. Only moments ago, the gym had been hot and steamy. But now, as gooseflesh rippled down my entire body, I shivered as if I'd been dipped in ice. Ashleigh walked these halls, sat in these classrooms, ate in this cafeteria, maybe danced in this gym.

"Are you still there?" Perry said.

"Yeah," I whispered.

"I was saying I'm going to do some more research. See if her graduating class has a page up anywhere. I want to find out as much about her time here in Eastport as I can."

"Okay, call me back if you find anything."

I ended the call and stared at the phone as if it were a foreign object. I'd never expected this turn of events. I searched the crowd for someone to tell. Justin and Mallory were out there on the dance floor having a great time. But I needed Gabriel. His father would want to know about this.

The sounds of screeching feedback shrieked through the gym. I winced. Others covered their ears. Someone yelled, "You suck," to the DJ.

The DJ smiled sheepishly, the microphone held tightly in his hand. "Now that I've got your attention," he said, and added a nervous laugh, "it's time for our Homecoming Court to lead us all in a dance."

I rolled my eyes. Tiffany's moment of glory. The chosen couples readied themselves to begin, but Brenden stood in the middle of the circle all alone and looking befuddled. I, along with the rest of the crowd, glanced around. Tiffany was nowhere to be found. Odd. Like she'd miss her chance at the spotlight.

I shook my head quickly and started searching for Gabriel again. I was done caring about that crowd and their dumb little dramas. I went out the double doors and into the hallway.

The school at night was like entering an alternate universe. Everything looked the same — the lockers, the classrooms. But the silence made it all feel different. Only half the lights were on. Many of the classroom doors were closed. There was no yelling, laughing, screeching. No crowd to push through. No slamming lockers. Only the dimly lit hall, the muted booming of the music from the gym, and the loud clicking of my heels on the floor.

My cell beeped. I pulled it out and looked at the screen. A text from Gabriel. He must have found his phone.

I opened the text, expecting something along the lines of how he found his phone and didn't need my help anymore and hey, by the way, did I choose between him and my first love yet? But, instead, there was simply one line:

meet me in the parking lot

Maybe he wanted to plead his case in private rather than in the crowded gym. Or maybe he'd changed his mind and realized he didn't have to wait around for me, he had his pick of countless girls here or at home. Home. Maybe he was going home. And he wanted to say good-bye.

In any case, I'd have to start talking before he did, because I didn't want to get into any of that now. I needed to tell him about Ashleigh. We needed to pass on the info to his dad at the police station.

I click-clacked down the hallway as fast as my heels could take me to the side exit. I pushed against the heavy metal door. The temperature had dropped since earlier and the sudden rush of cold air against my bare skin was a shock to my system. I rubbed my exposed arms and shoulders while I peered at the darkness.

My eyes were taking their sweet time to adjust from the lights of the school. The parking lot was spread out and Gabriel's text was kind of vague, so I headed toward a cluster of cars parked beneath one of the few light poles. I might not be able to see Gabriel, but he'd see me all lit up if I stood under that.

But I'd only taken a few steps in that direction when I heard a quickening of footsteps behind me. Before I could turn, strong arms wrapped around me from behind, and a damp rag was clamped over my mouth. It smelled sickly sweet with undertones of something chemical. I twisted and struggled, but it was like I was moving in slow motion. The light pole I'd focused on was blurring and swaying. And then I was flying through the air, my feet dangling, my left arm hanging lifeless. No, not flying, I realized. I was being carried.

I was gently laid into a trunk, my limbs bouncing off something familiar. A face hovered over the trunk like an angel of death. I squinted, trying to see who it was, but my mind was too fuzzy with shock and chemicals, and my eyes closed involuntarily. I tried to inch away, but that big familiar thing was next to me and it wouldn't budge.

The last thing I remembered before the darkness swallowed me was that the familiar thing beside me, touching my skin, felt a lot like a person. A body.

THIRTY-FOUR

THE FIRST SENSE THAT RETURNED WAS TOUCH. I was surprisingly comfortable. There was a firm softness beneath my whole body. I was sitting up, leaning back on something, I realized. And even though my mind was yelling, "OPEN YOUR EYES," I was so tired and comfy that I didn't want to quite yet.

But my hearing returned next. I heard panicked, rapid breathing and muffled sobs. I was so curious — despite the lure of my comfy cloud — that I opened my eyes.

My vision was blurred. It was dark, but bright light under the closed door leaked into the room, casting shadows on the plain white walls. I leaned forward. I was in a big chair. Some little voice in the back of my mind was screaming, but I didn't understand why she was scared.

I sat up straight and the room whooshed in and out like a zoom lens. My limbs tingled. I was still so tired. I considered closing my eyes again, but that muffled cry got louder, more insistent, so instead I craned my neck to look around the small room.

I squinted at a girl in a chair, her mouth covered, her hands and feet bound. *I know her*, I thought hazily. Her eyes widened and she bounced against the ropes that held her to the chair. She wanted my help. *Yeah, something's wrong here*, I thought. *Where am I again?*

That tiny voice in the back of my mind got louder and my heart started to speed up. I had a flash of myself waiting outside in the cold parking lot for Gabriel. The chemical-smelling rag over my face. The dark trunk. The body beside me.

I remembered it all in one giant injection of terror.

The text from Gabriel. No. My mind put it together now. Gabriel had lost his phone . . . And my stalker had swiped it and sent me the text to trick me into going outside.

I remembered I wasn't alone and stood up to help the girl in the chair. My legs wobbled as I tried to get my balance.

"I was drugged," I whispered to her apologetically. Though she was the last person on earth who deserved my help.

Tiffany nodded quickly. Up close I could see her eyes were red and puffy. Black mascara streaks ran down her cheeks. I remembered wondering why she'd missed her big moment as the Homecoming Court was called to the dance floor. She'd been taken already. Tossed in the trunk.

Adrenaline rushed through my body, giving me strength and clearing the clouds left behind from whatever had been on that rag. I quickly untied the gag and pulled it from Tiffany's mouth.

"What's going on?" she asked in a whisper-scream. "Someone kidnapped us!"

"I know," I whispered. "I'm going to get us out of here."

The room was small and plain-looking, with nothing on the walls. There was only an empty closet, a desk, my comfy chair, and the hard chair Tiffany was tied to. Also, no windows. What kind of room had no windows?

Wait. My eyes returned to the desk, and a sick realization came over me.

It wasn't just a desk. It was *the* desk. The dark cherry wood one in my vision. The one Sierra had written her note on. Sierra had been in this room.

My stalker was Sierra's killer. It wasn't a harmless person with creepy social skills. It was a deranged killer. Who'd first murdered Ashleigh Reed. Then Sierra Waldman. And now, he had me.

"Why are you just standing there?" Tiffany said. "Do something!"

I had to focus. I slipped out of my heels and padded across the rug to the door. I reached out for the knob.

"Be quiet about it," Tiffany pleaded.

I nodded, then tried to turn the knob slowly. "It's locked."

I looked around, but there was no sign of my purse. He must have taken it away or left it in the parking lot.

"Do you have your cell?" I asked.

Tiffany shook her head. Her chest rose and fell quickly as her breaths started to come faster. "He's going to kill us. We're going to die in here."

"We're not," I said. "We'll figure something out before he gets back."

"I can't believe this is happening. Who would do this?" Tiffany said between deep, painful-sounding breaths.

"Please, Tiffany, be quiet."

"Why did he tie me up, but he didn't tie you up?"

I was wondering the same thing, but shushed her. "I don't want him to hear us and come back. I need more time."

"He's going to . . . chop us up . . . kill us . . ." Tiffany was hyperventilating now, her breaths coming in ragged spurts between gory details of our soon-to-come violent deaths.

I leaned forward and slapped her across the face. Probably a bit harder than I needed to, but it worked. The slap shocked her into silence and she stopped her hysterical babbling.

"Panicking isn't going to help us," I said. "We have to come up with a strategy." I loosened the ropes around her ankles and hands. "Keep your arms behind you. Pretend you're still tied if he comes in."

I stood and gazed around the room. There was a closet in the corner. It was locked, but the knob was one of those flimsy, cheap ones. I yanked a pin out of Tiffany's hair.

"Ouch!"

I shushed her again and got to work. The lock turned easily and I swung the door open. The closet held only one thing: a box. I slid it out and took the top off. I was hoping for a gun or a phone or something useful, but it contained only mementos — like ticket stubs and dried flowers.

"We have nothing to use as a weapon," Tiffany said with some semblance of calm finally leaking into her voice.

"I have one thing." To give us a chance to get out of this alive, I had to get into the killer's head. Understand his insanity.

I worked quickly, giving each item only five to ten seconds before I gave up and moved on to the next. I picked up a dead pressed rose and a vision floated to the surface, dim and yellowed like old newspaper. I saw a girl spinning in a flowing skirt. We were at a school dance together. I held a rose in my hand that I couldn't wait to give to her. The long blond hair matched Perry's description of Ashleigh, but even without that, I'd have known it was her. I was overwhelmed with strong feelings. I adored her. She was the only thing that mattered to me. The only thing that got me through each day at this hellhole of a school. I worried slightly about what would happen after we graduated, but pushed the thought away. We'd be together forever. By the way Ashleigh returned my smile, I knew she loved me, too. I just hoped that love would never die.

The vision evaporated. I put the rose back down and sifted through a few other items until I picked up a red headband. An image rushed forward. Clearer and fresher than the other. I was watching Sierra, alone in the music room at school, playing the piano. She was so unbelievably talented, she took my breath away. This was the first time I'd felt so sure about someone since Ashleigh.

Sierra needed me. She had no friends. Her parents ignored her. I would take care of her. I walked up behind her and softly caressed her hair.

She jumped and the music abruptly stopped. *"Oh, it's you,"* she said with a nervous smile.

"I hope you don't mind that I was listening."

That voice. I knew that voice. I didn't want to focus too much on it, though, and pull out of the vision. If I could just hear it one more time.

"Of course not," Sierra said, blushing and twirling a strand of hair around her index finger.

"Are you still coming tonight? To my house like we planned?"

She straightened and pursed her lips. Trying to look older, sexy. *"I can't wait."*

"You're special, you know." I placed the headband on her head. She smiled at my little gift. She was so appreciative of any scrap of attention I gave her. I loved that about her. *"You're amazing."*

The vision ended with a jolt as he'd let go of the headband, and I realized why I recognized the voice. Who he was. But I didn't want to believe it.

"What?" Tiffany said, realizing from my gasp that I'd discovered something.

"It's Mr. Rylander." My voice sounded small and far away.

Tiffany's mouth opened in silent surprise. I needed to focus on a solution, a way out, but all I kept thinking was how shocked I was. And how all the pieces fit.

Mr. Rylander was the one Sierra began spending all her time with once she started school. I remembered seeing the tests in her bedroom. The low scores in math but perfect in science. Maybe he'd tutored her and that's how it started.

He'd been attracted to Sierra because she was astonishingly talented, like Ashleigh had been. But then things took a turn somewhere. Maybe she changed her mind and he killed her. Like he'd killed Ashleigh.

That's why Ashleigh broke through when Perry was doing the reading for Sierra's mother. Perry could usually contact a spirit only when they were connected to the person he was with. But Ashleigh never came through clearly. The connection was thin. She didn't know Mrs. Waldman. She didn't know me. But she knew what her ex-boyfriend was up to. And she'd tried to warn us. She came through the loudest as Perry and I drove past Rylander's cottage and I had my car accident. As Rylander was putting his trash can in his truck to take to the dump.

I covered my mouth with my hands. Sierra's body was found in the dump. He was probably loading her when we came crashing through his fence.

Ashleigh tried. She tried hard to stop it from happening again. But now I was here, in his room. A science teacher could easily get his hands on a chemical that would render a person unconscious, like what had been on the rag in the parking lot. I always knew he'd been a student at Eastport High. That day he'd told me about how he was also bullied, I thought he was showing concern, not bonding over our similarities. I thought about some of his lectures in class and how sometimes I felt they were meant for me. When he spoke of magnetism and attraction, I'd been thinking about Justin and Gabriel. And when he'd spoken of momentum and things put in motion that could not be stopped, I'd thought he was talking about my own life. He was . . . but just in a different way. I'd misread my own instincts.

Tiffany was still babbling incoherently. I could barely hear her through the rush of blood in my ears. If I wanted to survive this, I had to pull myself together. Screaming would do nothing. Assuming we were in Rylander's house on Cottage Row, there was no one around us in the off-season. Giving us no chance for rescue. At the dance, they might not have even realized I was missing yet. No one knew where I was.

"I need to tell you something," Tiffany said insistently. "I don't want to die without telling you the truth."

"We're not going to die," I said, rubbing my forehead.

"The night I hooked up with Justin —"

I put my hand up to stop her. "I don't want to hear this again. We're locked in a psychopath's room. We don't have time to fight about —"

"We didn't have sex," Tiffany blurted.

My mouth opened, but nothing came out. Thoughts rushed and collided so furiously through my head that I couldn't even string words together to make a sentence.

When I didn't speak, Tiffany continued, "We just kissed and then he passed out. While he was sleeping, I took his clothes off. When he woke up the next morning, I told him we'd had sex."

I drew each word out slowly. "Why would you do that?"

"To get back at Perry for humiliating me. I really liked him and he just used me and dropped me. If I couldn't hurt him, hurting his sister was the second best thing. It was an awful, kind of insane thing to do." She paused and let out a choked sob. "I'm sorry. Not just because we're going to die here together, but because it was a terrible thing. And I let both of you go on thinking it was worse than it was." She looked up at me with wet eyes.

It had never happened. I'd cried so many nights. Felt humiliation. Dumped Justin. Hated him for months. Over something that had never happened.

"What do you expect me to do now?" I snapped. "Give you a hug and say all is forgiven?"

"No, I just . . . I needed to confess in case —"

"We're not going to die. Not if you shut up and let me think."

I couldn't process the truth about her and Justin. This wasn't the time or place for it, so I hid it away in a little drawer in the back of my mind, marked DEAL WITH LATER.

I had to find a way to save my life first.

I brought my palms up to the side of my head, trying to think above the throbbing.

"I hear footsteps," Tiffany whispered. "He's coming."

Tiffany assumed her position on the chair. I shoved the box back into the closet, returned to my chair, and sat straight up.

The lock jiggled as a key was inserted. Then a click. My senses were amplified. My fingers tingled, gripping the upholstery beneath them. My heart hammered loudly from within my chest. The door slowly creaked open and the shaft of light from the hallway blinded my widened eyes. Then it slammed shut quickly, and we were once again plunged into darkness. I willed myself to slow my breathing.

He was inside. With us.

THIRTY-FIVE

WHILE WE WERE STILL IN DARKNESS, MY MIND struggled for a plan. I went with my gut.

"Hi, Mr. Rylander," I said, feigning confidence.

The light turned on. I squinted against the sudden brightness.

Rylander glanced quickly at Tiffany, then turned to give me his full attention. "You knew it was me?"

I gave a light shrug. "Of course."

"And you're not afraid?"

I stayed completely still, though my heart was pounding wildly in my rib cage, like it was trying to break free. "Do I have reason to be?"

He took a step toward me, looking pleased with my response. "I realize this was an unusual start to our relationship, but traditional beginnings are overrated. And you are definitely not a traditional girl." He chuckled. "I even had to wear gloves and use various other methods to hide my identity from you during the wooing process. That was a first. But I wanted my unveiling to wait until the time was right." He smiled. "I've looked for you for a long time, Clare."

Icy fingers crawled up my spine. Rylander took one step closer. I tried not to shudder. Not to show my disgust.

"I never had much luck with girls," he said. "Most of them are just so . . . average."

"Ashleigh wasn't," I said. "Sierra wasn't."

His eyes widened at my knowledge. "But Ashleigh betrayed me in Paris, and Sierra changed her mind after it was too late. They disappointed me in the end. You're not going to disappoint me, though, are you?"

I shook my head, too terrified to speak. My confidence was breaking and I was afraid that if I spoke, he'd know it was all faked.

He'd said the same things to Sierra that he'd written in his notes to me. I was talented. Unique. Special. Amazing. Just his type. Ashleigh had painting, Sierra had music, and I had my gift. I remembered the research Gabriel had done on delusional stalkers and their fantasy worlds. And how when things don't go the way they plan and the victim of their obsession doesn't live up to expectations . . . they turn violent.

I made myself talk.

"I won't disappoint you," I said. My voice was calm, while inside, my stomach churned.

"You wore the dress I bought you."

I forced the words out of my mouth. "Yes. I love it."

"Let us go!" Tiffany yelled suddenly.

He narrowed his eyes and dismissed her with a loud "Shut up!"

When he was faced the other way, I shook my head at her.

I hoped she got the message. *Stay quiet. Let me handle this. Let me play his game. It's the only way.*

Tiffany was nothing to him. He looked at her how she'd always looked at me — with hate, disdain, and condescension. I didn't know why he'd abducted Tiffany, but it was obvious she and I were there for very different reasons.

Rylander moved forward again, only a couple feet away from me now. "I was just like you, you know. In high school. I had my own Tiffanys and Codys. Every day, I endured the pain they inflicted on me. The name-calling. Books being knocked out of my hands. Slammed into lockers. Tripped while walking down the aisle in class. Mocked. Laughed at. Every. Single. Day."

"But you had Ashleigh," I said.

"Until she found someone else, in Paris." A shadow flickered over his face. "That was a terrible time for me. For a long time after, I stayed alone, not willing to let anyone else in. Not wanting to risk the hurt. But then, when I was ready, I set out to try again. To find someone just as special. Sierra was a misjudgment, but you . . ." He paused, considering me. "Do you know how special you are, Clare?"

"Yes, I do," I said automatically, wanting to agree with anything he said.

"It took some trial and error," he said. "And I made mistakes along the way. But I've found you now. And together we're going to be so happy. I'll prove it to you."

He turned, suddenly, and swooped over to Tiffany's side, his hand gesturing at her with a flourish. "You're probably wondering what *she's* doing here. Well, this is another gift for you."

I tilted my head to the side. "I don't understand."

"Just like the cockroach in her locker and the damage to Cody Rowe's car. They all messed with you, so I messed with them. But those were just small tokens. I saved the greatest gift for last. Tiffany has caused you the most trouble, so she gets to be my biggest offering."

He reached behind his back and pulled something free from his belt. It sliced through the air as he brought it down to his side. A knife. One of those large kinds they show on late-night infomercials that can effortlessly cut through impossible things.

Rylander grinned wickedly. "I'm going to kill her for you."

Tiffany's eyes pleaded with me for answers. I was the leader here. I had to figure out what to do. I gritted my teeth and moved to the edge of the chair. Rylander looked uncertainly at me.

"That girl," I said, pointing at Tiffany with a crooked finger. "Made my life a living hell."

Rylander nodded. "I know."

I dredged up every ounce of hatred I'd ever felt for Tiffany. Every moment I'd wished terrible things on her. I let all the anger bleed into my voice. "I never did *anything* to her and she ruined my life!" I yelled. "She turned people against me. She made my boyfriend betray me. She humiliated me every day. She made my life lonely and miserable!"

Rylander nodded eagerly with each word. "That's why it's the perfect gift."

My eyes bored into Tiffany. "No." I shook my head slowly. "It's not enough. I want more."

Rylander blinked quickly. "What do you want?"

I stood slowly, still a little unsteady on my feet. I held out my hand, palm up. "I want to be the one to do it. I want to kill her myself."

Rylander's eyes gleamed with pleasure at the thought. "Are you sure?"

My eyes slid to his. "Promise me we won't get caught?"

"We won't," he answered quickly. "We can put her somewhere they'll never find her. And if they do, we can run away. Together. And they'll never find us."

I stepped forward with forced confidence. "Let's do this."

Rylander licked his lips and held out the knife, greedy bloodlust in his eyes. I reached out and took it, the wooden handle heavy in my hand. For a moment, it felt like everything in me froze. As if even my blood stopped rushing through my veins.

I thought about the events of the last few days and wished I could have pieced things together sooner. Maybe then, I wouldn't be standing here with a knife and a girl's life in my hands. Every muscle in my body tightened in preparation for what I was about to do.

For what I *had* to do.

I raised the knife above my shoulder. Tiffany looked up at me with widened eyes and trembling lips. And with all my strength, I plunged the knife down.

I let go and scrambled backward, pulling Tiffany up off the chair and with me. Rylander screamed in agony as he looked down. The knife stuck out from his thigh. His eyes flashed toward me, burning with a horrifying rage. I was the one. He'd been sure of it. He'd picked correctly this time. But I, too, betrayed him.

I yanked open the door and ran into an all-gray room. The floor, walls, everything was cement. My first thought was that we were in some kind of dungeon, but then I realized it was the cottage's basement. That's why the room had no windows. Tiffany pushed me toward the right where she spotted the staircase. We sprinted up the stairs and burst onto the main floor. So close to escape. I felt lightheaded and slightly delirious from the rush.

The front door had a complicated system of bolts and locks. Tiffany tore at each one and pulled on the door. Still locked. She shrieked and tried again. Rylander was loudly limping up the stairs, gaining on us.

"Come on," I said, jumping impatiently in place. "He's coming!"

"I'm trying!" she squealed.

Rylander roared from behind us. I looked over my shoulder and saw him pulling the knife out of his leg, his face twisted in pain and anger. Blood poured from the wound. I hoped he'd drop, unconscious, but couldn't count on it.

"There's no time. Come on!" I grabbed Tiffany and pulled her into the bathroom. I closed and locked the door behind us.

"We'll go out there." I pointed to a half-size bathroom window, big enough for us to squeeze through one at a time.

Tiffany unlocked it and struggled to pull up the sill. "It's painted shut!"

I opened the medicine cabinet and rummaged through it, looking for anything we could use. I tore the blade out of Rylander's razor. Handing it to her, I said, "Use this. I'll stand at the door."

Rylander tried the handle, then began kicking at the door.

The wood was cheap and thin. Even *I* could kick it in, given enough time. "Work quickly," I said, as if that wasn't obvious.

Tiffany dug at the bottom of the sash with the blade as Rylander kicked and kicked.

Tremors shook my entire body, and my heart still pounded like a fist in my chest, but not from terror. My fear had been pushed to the background, overcome by a newer, stronger emotion: anger.

"You're making me do this!" Rylander yelled as he continued to kick.

I'd done it. I'd disappointed him. Just like all the others.

And he'd disappointed me.

His next kick splintered the wood, and the door burst open. But I was ready for him. I reared back my left arm and punched him as hard as I could. He staggered back, his eyes immediately watering as blood trickled between the fingers that had involuntarily risen to his nose. I wanted to strike again before he regained his composure. I lifted my knee up high, ready to give him a snap kick to the groin. But his arm lashed out, grabbing my foot before I could make contact, and twisting it to an impossible angle. I cried out in pain. My hands reached out to brace my fall as the floor came rushing up to meet me.

As my world was literally turning upside down, I saw Tiffany, her body already halfway out the window. Then Rylander, still holding my foot, started pulling me backward. I flailed at the floor, trying to dig my fingernails into the grout between the tiles, but it was no use. I screamed as excruciating pain radiated up from my ankle, making my whole leg go numb.

This was it. I was being dragged to my death. Fear returned in the form of a giant weight on my lungs. I couldn't breathe. My heart constricted and I felt an overwhelming sense of failure. I'd lost. I was going to die here. When I still had so much left I wanted to do.

Then, seemingly out of nowhere, Tiffany sprang forward, gouging at Rylander's face and eyes with her long fingernails. She knocked him backward. He tripped over the wreckage of the shattered door and slammed down to the floor, hitting headfirst. He was out cold.

"Go! Go!" Tiffany yelled as I scrambled up and pulled myself through the window, barely registering the new pain from my arms. I fell to the grass below and Tiffany soon followed. She pulled me up and began to run.

Adrenaline gave me the strength to do a limping trot through the side yard, toward the front. Tiffany was screaming her head off, but that wouldn't help us if no one else was on the street. I didn't know how long Rylander would be out. He might have already regained consciousness.

White-hot pain shot up from my ankle, but I pushed on

while Tiffany yelled, "Faster, faster," over her shoulder. She skidded to a stop at the sight of a car careening into the driveway.

"It's Perry!" I yelled.

He jumped out of the driver's side and started toward us.

I waved my arms at him. "Get back in! We've got to go!"

Tiffany tore open the back door and pushed me in, then toppled in beside me. She screamed at Perry to go and grabbed his phone to dial 9-1-1 as the smell of burning rubber lit up the street.

THIRTY-SIX

TWO DAYS AFTER I FOUGHT OFF A CRAZED KILLER
and saved the life of my mortal enemy, I lay on the couch, my
ankle propped up on pillows. I took inventory of my injuries.
My left hand was swollen, the knuckles cut. Scratches lined
the underside of my arms from pulling myself out the window. My ankle was severely sprained and I'd need crutches
for a little while. But I was alive.

Tiffany was also fine. We hadn't spoken since we gave our
statements at the police station that night. I had no interest in
being friends with her, but she'd come back and saved me
when it counted. So maybe a peace treaty of some sort was in
order.

Perry had continued his Ashleigh research when we'd gotten off the phone. He'd found her graduating class online and
sifted through the photos uploaded there. And found one of
her with a younger Mr. Rylander. It had all clicked into place
for Perry then, especially why Ashleigh had gone bananas
right in front of Rylander's house. And that's how Perry had
known where I was.

I spent all Saturday night in the ER and the police station. I spent all of Sunday drifting in and out of painkiller-induced sleep. I heard the phone and the doorbell, often, but Mom wouldn't let anyone in to see me. I needed my rest, she'd repeat to anyone who tried.

Now, Monday, everyone else was in school, though I doubted there would be any learning today. They'd probably do an assembly to tell everyone about The Secret Life of Mr. Rylander the Psycho. Word about what Tiffany and I had gone through had probably spread like wildfire. They'd calm the student body down, tell them Rylander was in police custody, and offer counselors.

Detective Toscano called a while ago to fill me in on more details. Rylander confessed to everything — from killing Ashleigh and Sierra to stalking me. He'd had a string of failed relationships with women before he returned to his hometown. Then he pursued Sierra, figuring she'd be easier to control since she was inexperienced and innocent. And instead of looking at him as a predator, she was naïvely flattered that a guy — a good-looking, smart, older guy — was interested in her. But at some point she'd had second thoughts. Unfortunately, too late.

After Sierra disappointed him, he'd set his sights on me. I was his type — uniquely talented with an extraordinary gift. And I was injured. Mentally. He knew how it felt to be bullied; he knew all about that pain. Maybe those experiences in high school were what made him lose his grip on reality, who knows. But, like a shark to an injured fish, he was attracted to me. Thinking I was weak. And that I'd understand him in a way others hadn't.

He'd met his match, all right.

"You still drugged out?" Perry asked, poking his head into the living room.

"No, I'm awake," I said, using my elbows to lift myself up a bit on the couch. "The pain's not so bad anymore. I switched to Motrin."

"That's good." He walked in, carrying a glass of milk and a sandwich on a TV tray. "Mom wanted me to see if you were hungry."

"Nah, not right now."

He bent forward, carefully placing the tray on the coffee table. "Maybe later, then." He straightened and looked at me, but didn't say anything.

"So." I pulled myself up to a sitting position to give him room at the end of the couch. "Any word from Ashleigh?"

"Not since you were saved," he said, sitting down carefully. "I think she's satisfied."

"And you managed to leave the house and be the hero. Who do you think you are, Spider-Man?"

I expected a chuckle, but he stayed serious.

"When I realized Rylander had been Ashleigh's high school boyfriend, I called you back," he said quietly. "You didn't answer and I started to worry. I called you again and again and realized something had happened. And . . . the anxiety . . . it was just gone. You were more important. Before I knew it, I was in the car, speeding toward Rylander's house."

"That doesn't mean you're cured."

"I know." He scratched at the fabric of the sofa, obviously hating this topic. "I told Mom. She's making me see someone." He rolled his eyes. "To talk about my feelings." Each word dripped with sarcasm.

"That's the right thing to do, Perry." I adjusted my position, grimacing at my sore ankle as I inched up a bit.

"Thanks for not giving up on me after I acted like such a jackass."

"Don't thank me," I said with mock indignation. "You're my brother. I'd never give up on you. You're the most important person in the world to me." I quickly added in a hushed voice, "Don't tell Mom. She'll be jealous."

Then he laughed, for the first time in a long time. It was the most wonderful sound I'd ever heard. And if my minor injuries had been the force that pushed him onto the road to recovery, then I'd wince happily.

Perry left to go call Nate and tell him how I was doing. Apparently, Nate had worriedly called for updates so many times that Mom temporarily banned him. As Perry walked away, he looked better than he had in months. Lighter, with his burden shared.

Perry thought I was the strong one, but I had a lot of fear. I'd feared letting Mallory in and nearly lost my chance at true friendship. I'd been frozen in my fear of hurting someone and that kept me from moving forward in my life. But it was time for all that to change. Hell, even Mom had a date planned next month for Phil's sister's wedding.

I glanced at my watch. School was out. I sent him a text:

can you come over

Almost immediately, my phone buzzed with his response: *be there in five*

I lifted myself up onto my crutches and hobbled out the front door. It was unseasonably warm. I eased myself onto the porch swing, wincing as I hefted my leg up to rest it on a wicker side table. I raised my face to the sun and closed my eyes, enjoying the warmth on my skin. Thoughts rushed through my head. The usual fearful ones.

Was I making the right decision?

I didn't want to hurt anyone.

I didn't want to regret this.

I'd had a lot of time, alone in my room, over the last day or so, to think. I thought about Tiffany's confession and the truth about Justin. I thought about Gabriel's ultimatum and my feelings for him. I thought about the past and the future. I thought about losing someone and hurting someone. And I decided that it was time to stop letting fear paralyze me. I'd take a risk. Follow my feelings instead of my careful calculations. And see what happened.

I'd been so lost in these thoughts that I didn't hear him coming up the porch steps until he stood right before me. He rushed forward and grabbed my hands.

"I'm so glad you're okay. I came by before, but your mom wouldn't let me see you."

I smiled. "Don't take it personally. She's been like the Secret Service since I got home."

"I'd feel that way, too." He paused and swallowed hard. "I wish I'd been able to protect you."

"It's done. It's in the past. And I'm so sick of the past." I hesitated for a moment, wanting to find just the right tone to convey the importance of my next few words. "I want to move forward." My eyes searched his, to see if he got my gist.

"Do you mean . . . ?"

I nodded and quickly asked, "Am I too late?"

"No. Definitely not."

He dropped to his knees before the porch swing, careful to avoid my outstretched leg. He slowly took my face in his hands and held it for a moment, looking deep into my eyes. Every part of me felt more alive — my heart sped up, my pulse raced, my skin tingled. I knew I'd made the right decision.

"Gabriel?" I said.

"Yeah?" His voice was breathless.

"Kiss me."

First he took in a sharp breath, then leaned in, his lips so gentle on mine. As if he worried that I was going to disappear.

I laced my fingers through the back of his hair and pulled him closer, which elicited a small moan from his mouth. He pulled back for a moment and just looked at me. Like I was going to change my mind or panic and run away. With a little smile, I drew him back in for another kiss.

I couldn't imagine my life without Justin in it, but I truly believed we were meant to be great friends. And that we could be. He'd need time to come to terms with my decision, but I knew he'd be better off with someone more like him. Someone who enjoyed the parties and the social scene that made him so happy. But that wasn't me. I am who I am, and I didn't want to force Justin to change, either. That would be like asking a star to dim its light.

And I owed it to myself to give this thing with Gabriel a chance. He'd blown into my life like a hurricane, turned me upside down, challenged me at every turn. And, together, we sparked like lightning.

Were Gabriel and I going to fall in love? Be together forever? Live our lives happily as soul mates? Who the hell knew something like that? I sure didn't. I can't see the future.

All I knew was that I would love finding out.

ACKNOWLEDGMENTS

Thanks to:

Everyone at Scholastic, but particularly Aimee Friedman, Lauren Felsenstein, and Nikki Mutch.

My agent, Scott Miller.

My family and outlaws.

My parents, Dan and Barbara Harrington.

My friends, both online and off.

Susan Happel Hooplehead Edwards.

Enthusiastic readers, booksellers, librarians, and bloggers.

And every moment of every day . . . Mike and Ryan.

You all know why.